PRAISE FOR *VERTIGO*

'Beautifully simple and unembellished . . . most captivating in its ability to unnerve.'

Claire Hazelton, *The Guardian*

'A psychological landscape lightly spooked by loneliness, jealousy and alienation.'

Heidi Julavits, *The New York Times*

'*Vertigo* is artful, intelligent . . . Walsh is a sublimely elegant writer.'

Sarah Ditum, *New Statesman*

'This collection makes the familiar alien, breaking down and remaking quotidian situations, and in the process turning them into gripping literature.'

Vol. 1 Brooklyn

'Walsh handles the seismic events of life . . . with a sort of alien bluntness and mania for category that forces her language into bizarre, thrilling new shapes.'

Left Bank Books, Staff Pick

'Simple but stunning in its precision.'

Music and Literature

'With wry humour and profound sensitivity, Walsh takes what is mundane and transforms it into something otherworldly with sentences that can make your heart stop. A feat of language.'

Kirkus, Starred Review

'Inventive, honest . . . a compelling pitch into the inner life.'

Publishers Weekly

'Splendidly wry and offbeat . . . both intellectual and aware. Stories to be digested slowly, and savoured.'

Lesley McDowell, *Sunday Herald*

PRAISE FOR *HOTEL*

'Joanna Walsh is fast becoming one of our most important writers. *Hotel* is a dazzling tour de force of embodied ideas.'

Deborah Levy, author of *Black Vodka*

'Subtle and intriguing, this small book is an adventure in form. Part meditation on hotels, it mingles autobiography and reflections on home, secrets, and partings. Freud, Dora, Heidegger, and the Marx Brothers all have their moments on its small, intensely evocative stage.'

Lisa Appignanesi, author of *Trials of Passion*

'It's a knockout. Completely engaging, juicy and dry – such a great book.'

Chris Kraus, author of *I Love Dick*

'Walsh's writing has intellectual rigour and bags of formal bravery . . . a boldly intellectual work that repays careful reading.'

Melissa Harrison, *Financial Times*

'[A] slyly humorous and clever little book ... [Walsh moves] effortlessly and imaginatively from one thing to the next . . . with utter conviction in each step.'

Marina Benjamin, *New Statesman*

'A slim, sharp meditation on hotels and desire.'

The Paris Review

'Evocative . . . Walsh's strange, probing book is all the more affecting for eschewing easy resolution.'

Publishers Weekly

'Underneath [her] clever wit and wordplay is a vein of melancholy . . . Walsh mixes travel writing, pop culture, and personal narrative to great effect.'

San Diego City Beat

WORLDS FROM THE WORD'S END

WORLDS FROM THE WORD'S END

Joanna Walsh

SHEFFIELD – LONDON – NEW HAVEN

First published in 2017 by And Other Stories
Great Britain – United States of America
www.andotherstories.org

Stories from this collection have appeared in different forms in: *The Berlin Quarterly* ('Two', 2016), *Narrative Magazine* ('Bookselves', 2014), Catapult.co ('Postcards from Two Hotels', 2015), *Best European Fiction* ('Worlds from the Word's End', 2015), *The Stinging Fly* ('Like a Fish Needs a . . . ', 2015), *Fractals* ('Exes', 'Femme Maison', 'Blue', 'Reading Habits' and 'Hauptbahnhof', 2013), *The Letters Page* ('Travelling Light', 2015), *Visual Verse* ('Dunnet', 2015), *#ShortStoryAnthology 1* ('Two Secretaries', 2015), *Granta* ('Enzo Ponza', 2015), *Hearing Voices* ('The Story of Our Nation', 2015), *Grow a Pair* ('Simple Hans', 2015), and *I Am Because You Are* ('Me and the Fat Woman – Joanna Walsh', 2015). 'The Suitcase Dog' was first published as an audio edition on vinyl by Visual Editions and Ace Hotels, 2015.

9 8 7 6 5 4 3 2 1

Material from *The Rediscovery of the Mind* by John R. Searle is used by permission of the publisher, The MIT Press.

ISBN: 978-1-911508-10-6
eBook ISBN: 978-1-911508-11-3

Typesetter: Tetragon, London; Typefaces: Linotype Swift Neue and Verlag; Cover Painting and Design: Roman Muradov; Printed and bound by the CPI Group (UK) Ltd, Croydon, CR0 4YY.

A catalogue record for this book is available from the British Library.

And Other Stories is supported by public funding from Arts Council England.

CONTENTS

TWO

It's time.

I have lined them up, the two of them, holding hands. Not that they need to be lined up as they are already pressed side by side in a way I have never been able to do anything about but it seems, at this moment, as if I have arranged them in this way quite deliberately, and that they stand here, exactly as I would wish they would, through some act of volition. They're spruced up and looking their best, as they should be, today of all days. They have never been out before, not like this, though I have to admit they have been out a couple of times before. Or more.

So, here they are. I have brought them here myself. They are not heavy but they are cumbersome. I have exhibited them here for many years unsure now what my arms, stretched from encircling them so long, will to do without them. I have kept them polished, but never like today. Today they are gleaming. They gleam so hard that sometimes it seems almost as if they wink at me – if it isn't sentimental to call them 'they' for 'they' are not what they seem. They only look like they; they are 'it'. Yes, to think of them otherwise would be sentimental. And I know very well it is not for their sake that I come here day after day. And it is not for their sake that I am giving them away.

Moreover, if I were to be honest, this sprucing up has happened not only on this day but on many. Nevertheless it makes me proud to see them standing here, hand in hand, the smaller one having begun so quickly and unexpectedly, while the bigger I already had by heart. The larger holds the other by the hand. They seem as if about to cross the road. I have spent years standing by the side of this road presenting what I have to no one, or only to the few cars that go by. It's my fault, I suppose, for having chosen such a road. There's no pavement, and all passers-by are in cars. Still it is the only road there is, to my knowledge, and I am perhaps lucky to be here at all. On the other hand there's nowhere to park and the traffic laws, expressed in solid lines painted by the kerbside, mean that drivers, even if they want to stop, must keep going. I'm not the only person here of course. There are vendors – of fruit and cold drinks, I think – who seem to make a living at it, though their stalls are located in lay-bys a little way off, while here I am standing on a narrow grass verge that backs onto a steep wall of rock, nowhere even for vehicles to turn. I did not think of these things early enough, the lay-bys I mean. When I passed the first time they were all occupied and, since then, all the times I have been here, I have had to keep on meekly offering them up from the place you see me now, which is not what I'd have chosen, had I been given any choice in the matter. My prospects may still be better elsewhere but it would take so much time to research and relocate that I might miss a chance, and I need only one chance. Even if I moved, knowing little of the area besides my own stretch of road, I would have no guarantee of a better venue. Perhaps it would be worse.

When I started it was spring, not this spring. I'm not sure which. It is not spring now. The weather has changed. It is still bright though the time of year is colder, and I must be careful describing the seasons as they may always also be mistaken for metaphor, and I would not like to lay down some kind of mood setting I didn't at all mean. My time here has not been a bad time though the weather sometimes has been. I even find myself wishing I had endured some harder times, rather than standing by the side of the road all year with my two polished and uncomplaining companions. Hard times would have given me something to think about while waiting, could even have given me the impetus to leave and go on to something better like the vendors of fruit and bottled water, who come and go as I do not. I have forbidden myself to think about their hard times because they are not my hard times. I am paralysed outside their hard times and with no way to go on towards them, or, rather, back. I am somewhere better than them already, though it is not so very good, not so good as I might have wished. Perhaps when another of them has gone, I may take over one of their positions.

But all that does not matter now, because on *this* day someone is coming for them, someone to whom I have wanted to give them away for a long while. 'To whom'? Who am I kidding? It is the wanting to give them away that has gone on for so long, but so few people have wanted them, if any. Yet now someone does. And I must give them up gratefully and with no fuss, so here they are.

I got the phone call yesterday evening. *Someone* said, they had seen me in passing, from their car. *Someone* said, they're just the thing I'm looking for. I was a little worried by the word 'thing', but they assured me they would treat them with care. *Someone* said they would meet me here, right on my usual spot, about this time. *Someone* described their car.

As someone is coming for them, I have made sure they are absolutely clean: their shiny cheeks, which are, perhaps, more shiny than ever before, their shiny clothes, which should not really be shiny, but there you are. Cleanliness, oh that matters too. No matter that they are both somewhat worn out and more so than ever with the shining that makes their limbs threadbare, almost through to the bone, which glistens in its own way, underneath.

Sometimes I have thought of getting rid of them by other means. Who wouldn't? So poised to move, yet so immobile, so lifelike and at the same time something that only looks like life, they are a burden. I have thought of destroying them, of pushing them into the road under the wheels of a car, or better, a juggernaut. I am angry with them as they do not move, but, if I hit them, I know that splinters will fly, nothing more. And then they will be damaged goods. I cannot present them damaged. I have learnt skills in order to polish and maintain them, and that would be a waste of all the time I spent learning, as well as the hard work. Still, sometimes I am angry, angry enough to push them under a car, or to wait for a truck, and I have imagined the air filled with tiny shards so small that they float like hay. But of course I have not done it, and I should not blame myself: everyone has these thoughts, or something like them. I have also thought of crossing the road – though this is dangerous because of the traffic at my corner – pitching them into the ditch on the far side, leaving them to rot. But I'm afraid they would continue to call for me, and I couldn't bear that for however long – the months, or longer – it took them to decompose. So I have thought these things, but I have not done them. I have lived with these thoughts for years. I comfort myself by saying that these thoughts are necessary to their survival, and perhaps to mine. Still, such violence! Even if unacted. Instead I wait, only a little tense, trying not to show it, whistling a tune or walking up and down my patch of grass, knowing how far to go, beyond which borders not to stray.

Despite my years standing here I still quietly believe that I cannot be seen, that no one will stop. I do not like to believe that people see me and do not stop, because I know they are good people. It is better to believe that I am insignificant, which perhaps I am. In truth I've no one to blame but myself.

I can't say nobody warned me, when I started on this one.

I hear two voices in my head: my mother who, finding herself in such a landscape, would surely exhibit delight, or something that looked like it; my father, who would be full of scorn. My mother would brush their cheeks, and exclaim, *how nice they look!* She would glance at the scrub growing on the cliff face and say, *What pretty flowers!* My father would grunt and turn away, as though to notice were itself disgusting. My parents made a big fuss the first time I took them out, so big that my mother's emotions cancelled out my father's, though not the noise they made in having them. At that time it was not usual for me to go out so I made a big fuss too, no doubt drew attention to myself, but how else could I have dealt with exiting? I don't know what my parents said about it. I didn't go back.

Well, that's all over now. But, when I am rid of them, then what?

It is a long time since I left my parents' house and preparing to die in a quite practical way is something I will have to think about for the new year. It is, I believe, the first time I will have had to think about it so practically, the first time it has seemed so practical a possibility. Of course it may happen before the new year, though I am not planning on that. The likelihood of death is something I will allow only after the year has flipped over and the dates begun again. I will not permit anything else so untidy. Of course this will mean that I will not be able to come here, every day, to offer them, not for them, not for just anyone who might want them. But that's OK because finally it's time.

For what – 'goodbye'? There is no what.

A car pulls in to the side of the road. It is the car that was described to me, an old car with a dent and a roof rack tied on with rope, which causes me a little worry but, having got this far without mishap, it is surely adequate. The car lists slightly as it takes the camber. I cannot see who is at the wheel. It slows, is about to stop, then something in it changes. It begins to speed up and disappears round the corner. I run a few steps (as though I could ever catch it), begin to wave (as though they could ever see me), then I look after it for seconds, for minutes (as though my gaze could pull it back!). It does not come back. I listen. I cannot hear it turning, returning. The thing is, I don't know if that was the right car. The thing is, I have to keep on looking. The thing is, we had an agreement, on the phone, so, though it looked like the car, it cannot have been. When I look back from the corner, there they are, not moving, just the same as they always were.

They cannot love me.

(I mean, it cannot love me.)

But looking into their little wooden eyes, I must believe it can.

BOOKSELVES

On your parents' bookshelves little comes and goes. Few books are added; old books are rarely taken down or away.

The relics of a more intense age of reading – of school, of university – their books are castaways, washed up on a beech of elegant shelves, evidence that your mother and father can still do it, or that they did it when they were young in the sixties when – suddenly – everyone was doing it but, being older now, it's understandable they don't do it so much any more.

You too once thought accumulation was achievement. But your shelves have no stability: books come and go with the frequency of phone calls, or of the phone calls we don't make nowadays.

Your parents still use the phone, as do their friends of that generation. When the phone rings your father shouts, not at your mother but at the space around her, 'Phone! Phone! Quick! Get the phone!' And your mother runs backwards and forwards from room to room looking, though the phone is in the same place it always is, then your father gets up and runs backwards and forwards looking and eventually, before either of them are able to answer it, the phone stops ringing.

Your phone travels with you in your pocket and, when your significant other gets in touch, it makes a buzzing sound. You never misplace it but you do misplace books, though when you want to lay your hands on one you do not shout, or have a wife to shout at or a husband to do the shouting at you, and the whole process is slower because you only have one phone but – books – you have so many.

They spill from your shelves. They sprawl by your bed, luxurious, splayed sometimes and discarded at an early page, broken by your attentions. On your shelf more books you would like to read are waiting, books you have ordered, their white bodies fat with potential. They are not the only books to oppress you. There are the books you would still like to buy – bookshops full of them – opening themselves into distant pale horizons that slide back endlessly into their gutters' slits, where they meet a barrier of card and paper. However deep the perspective, you can make only a needle's-width of entry, the width of a spine. It hardly seems worth the trouble; there are so many to conquer. Still they do not accuse you urgently enough. Nor do the books you take home from the bookshop but neglect, though you have many times imagined – so vividly – sitting down with one of them at your table (situated conveniently adjacent to your bookshelf) that it is scarcely worth the bother of enacting the scene. Your books lie primed to spring, ever solicitous of your attention.

Something you never thought might happen: after a certain number of years the being who has read all these neglected books will step from your bookshelves, will sit down at your table (conveniently adjacent), will make a cup of coffee at the machine, having seen you use it so many times, especially when about to tackle a book, and will light a cigarette, insubstantial as steam, the odour of which will affect neither your carpets nor curtains. It will be the opposite of you, your inverse.

You will come downstairs at midnight, looking for a glass of water, and find it there. Although surprised, you will not call the police, set off the fire alarm, scream, 'Stop, thief!' You will recognise 'it' instantly, shamefacedly, though you will not be able to say whether 'it' is 'he' or 'she'. You will have no opportunity to retreat, or to fail to confess your guilt, which you will see reflected, instantly, in its hollow eyes. Unable to think of an excuse to leave, you will fall into conversation warily. At first you will attempt to entertain it but your bookself will appear to find you trivial, its nose deep in some tome.

You will take down a volume and try to show it who's boss. Your choice will be, perhaps, *Journey to the End of the Night* in the original French, a book you have only previously attempted when drunk. You will be annoyed to find your copy unpredictably well-thumbed as well as casually stained with something brown and sticky, once liquid. Your bookself reads, not like you, but like an ideal reader. Little distracts it. It holds its paperback between thumb and index finger. Its large, knob-knuckled claw dominates the volume single-handed, casually as a cigarette, a cocktail. As it curls the cover of the paperback against its spine, you watch in silent fury. Sitting opposite you set your book flat on the table, elbows weighting its edges to prevent lift-off. When you imitate your bookself's poise, your book rebels, splutters from your fingers in a spree of pages.

However.

After some time spent reading together a surprising thing will happen: a secret feeling of superiority will begin to grow within you. You will recognise your bookself's habit of opening a work some way from the beginning, at the exact point, indeed, that you lost interest and, furthermore, of reading on but stopping short of the very last page. Your confidence will increase as you discover it has devoured all the books you have thrown aside: ill-judged gifts from well-meaning relatives; friends' recommendations you have loathed from the very first page; gardening manuals; thick books of instructions for obsolete electrical devices; the memoirs of politicians. It has been through the charity bag. It has scraped every word from torn and mouldering volumes streaked with tea and bacon fat at the bottom of the dustbin.

You will begin to pity its terrible appetite.

Your growing feeling of superiority will generate within you at first a patronising empathy that will lead you to quiz it. But, as you discover how much information your bookself possesses that you do not, your mood will first change to grudging respect then to genuine interest.

You will sit down together, friendly now, to exchange information, opinions. You will switch from coffee to alcohol and offer your bookself a glass. Conspiratorially, you will admit you have neglected its areas of knowledge. Your bookself will be strangely wistful for all those missed pages, all those openings, all those endings.

After several more glasses of whisky or wine or beer, you will lead your bookself to your bookshelves, which after years of accumulation reach, like those of your parents, from floor to ceiling. You will feel you are showing it a kingdom, a new horizon that will, uniquely in your joint presence, unfold for both of you at the same instant, its peeling wall of spines curling with aged contracted glue revealing – not a beach – but a forest of yellowing bound signatures which will part, flopping like flaccid palm trees. In the cracks beyond them will be only dark. You will feel that, if you could break through, together, you might . . . well . . . break *through* the paper to the words and then through the words to . . . to . . . whatever. Your bookself will have the same idea. You will hand your bookself book after book until its insubstantial arms are spilling but then (perhaps it was the whisky or the wine or beer or whatever your tipple) you will remember the book, the one book, that it absolutely must read and (after all your tastes are not so dissimilar) you will begin to search for it, to pull books down in handfuls. Though you both know the book (which you too have not read, but had always intended to), neither of you will be able to quite remember the title or to identify its author. Books will fly to the floor past, no through, your bookself, rending, abandoning, abstracting themselves until the shelves are as bare and as yellow as sand, until behind the bookshelves there is nothing to be seen but woodchip wallpaper, slightly discoloured, a tidemark of dust showing the height limit of your erstwhile library.

You will both sit down in your disaster of bookshelves, to contemplate their ruins. You will agree: had you always the right book to hand, oh what reading you would have done!

Only after a few more glasses of wine (or beer or whisky), will you both admit that, after all, perhaps you do not really like books.

POSTCARDS FROM TWO HOTELS

THE FIRST HOTEL

I

The first hotel is expensive; I am not paying for it.

There are notepads by the pillows; the chair is far too low for the desk.

II

Small things disappear: this is normal.

The towels are changed although I do not put them in the tub.

III

Schedule: 'Down time at the hotel'.

(No further instructions.)

IV

I run the bath, pile my books by the bath, get in.

Once in I do not read my books.

V

I get out. Something in the room had changed: perhaps it is the distances.

It is easy to lose things in a blank space.

VI

I regret:

A tiny phial of perfume.

Some hairpins.

VII

I am told always:

Outside the hotel, things are getting worse.

I don't speak the language.

VIII

Inside the door: three locks.

And:

'If the smoke is heavy, seal the door with wet towels.'

IX

Things I should have brought with me:

An umbrella.

Things I should have brought with me:

Pyjamas.

X

The hotel safe growls when it closes. It acquiesces when opening.

'As a courtesy, we will brilliantly shine your shoes.'

Joanna Walsh

THE SECOND HOTEL

I

The second hotel is further out. It is still within the city.

The outskirts are safer than the centre: it's beyond I'm told to worry about most.

II

The notepads, also by the pillow, are smaller.

The towels are threadbare: I try to ignore this.

III

The chair is also too low for the desk; the safe does not work.

As in the last hotel, I rearrange my small possessions constantly.

IV

There are two bottles of water in the bathroom.

(In the first hotel there was only one.)

In both hotels, booked into a double room, I remain single.

V

I close the bedside drawer. I go into the bathroom.

I return. The drawer is open. I close the drawer.

VI

The toiletries are named after the city of the last hotel.

It is only when I get to the second hotel that I miss the first.

VII

The mosquito screen slides across the window.

The window slides across the mosquito screen.

VIII

In the courtyard, the birds swallow their voices, which I do not recognise.

I can hear the ring road. Some things still cannot prevent themselves from being beautiful.

IX

There is no one in the swimming pool.

A small piece of skin from my foot flakes onto the floor. I *will* not have a bad time here.

X

Tomorrow I return to the first hotel.

It is in the second hotel that I did all my writing.

WORLDS FROM THE WORD'S END

We need to talk.

I'm writing to you so you'll understand why I can't write to you any more.

I could never talk to you. We didn't exactly have a meaningful relationship. Perhaps that's why I have all these words left when so many others have none at all. The postal system's still going so I expect you will get this letter. Bills continue to be sent by mail (figures accompany icons: an electric light bulb, a gas flame, a wave for water) as do postcards (wordless views). And letters do still arrive so I'll take this opportunity to get my words in edgeways while I can, folded into a slim envelope. When they drop through your letterbox, I hope that they don't fall flat.

It's the old story: It's not you, it's me. Or, rather, it's the place we're at. We don't talk any more, not now, not round here. You know how things have changed. But I have to tell you all over again because what happened between us seemed to be part of what happened everywhere. It's never useful to lay the blame but I do feel somehow responsible.

It was more than a language barrier. We were reading from the same page, at least that's what I thought, but it was really only you that ever had a way with words. Sometimes you put them into my mouth, then you took them right out again. You never minced them, made anything easier to swallow, and the words you put in for me were hardly ever good. They left a bitter taste. As for mine, you twisted my words and broke my English until I was only as good as my word: good for nothing, or for saying nothing. I stopped answering and that was the way you liked it. You told me you preferred your women quiet. You studied the small ads: *INCREASE YOUR WORD POWER!* Trouble was, you didn't know your own strength.

Communication went out of fashion about the same time as we stopped speaking. It started, as does almost everything, as a trend. Early adapters, seeking something retro as usual, looked to their grannies, their aunties: silent women in cardigans who never went out. Who knows if these women were really quiet? Whether their adoption of these women's silence was a misinterpretation of the past or a genuine unearthing, it happened. Initially gatherings – I mean parties, that sort of thing – became quieter, then entirely noiseless. Losing their raison d'être, they grew smaller and eventually ceased to exist altogether in favour of activities like staying in, waiting in hallways at telephone tables for calls that never came.

We scarcely noticed how the silence went mainstream but if I have to trace a pattern I'd say our nouns faded first. In everyday speech the grocery store became 'that place over there'; your house, 'the building one block from the corner, count two along.' A little later this morphed into, 'that place a little way from the bit where you go round, then a bit further on'. We began to revel in indirectness. Urban coolhunters would show off, limiting themselves to 'that over there,' and finally would do no more than grunt and jerk a thumb. They looked like they had something better to do than engage in casual conversation. We provincials were dumbstruck.

Grammar went second. We tried abbreviations, acronyms, but they made us blue, reminded us of the things we used to say. Not being a literary nation, we'd never quite got our heads around metaphor, and our frequent grammatical errors were only one thing less to lose. We said 'kinda' a lot, and 'sort of' but, y'know . . . We lost heart and failed to end sentences.

We have no sayings, now, only doings, though never a 'doing word'. Actions speak louder than words (a wise saw: if only I'd looked before I ever listened to you), especially as we can't remember very far back. We have erased all tenses except the present, though for a while we hung on to the imperfect, which suggested that things were going on as they always had done, and would continue thus.

At least schooling is easier now there are only numbers and images – and shapes, their dimensions, their colours. We don't have to name them: we feel their forms and put them into our hearts, our minds, or whatever that space is, abandoned by language. We trace the shapes of the countries on school globes with our fingertips. And they all feel like tin.

Being ostensibly silent, for a while social media was still a valid form of communication, though touch-keyboards began to be preferred to those with keys. On websites, people posted photos of silent activities, as well as those involving white noise – drilling, vacuuming, using the washing machine – during which communication could patently not take place. Some questioned, in the comments boxes below, whether these photos might be staged but doubts were put to rest when the majority began to frown even on the use of writing. Some of us wondered whether internet forums could have themselves been the final straw: the way we'd wanted what we said to be noticed and, at the same time, to remain anon: the way we'd let our words float free, detach from our speech acts, become at once our avatars and our armour.

Trad media was something else. The first to go 'non-talk' were high-end cultural programmes: those 'discussing' movies and books. Popular shows featuring, say, cooking, gardening, home improvement, and talent contests, relied on sign language and were frowned upon by purists. On highbrow broadcasts, critics' reactions were inferred from their facial expressions by a silent studio audience. Viewers smiled or frowned in response but their demeanours remained subtle, convoluted, suited to the subjects' complexities. Fashions in presenters changed. Smooth-faced women were sacked in favour of craggy hags whose visual emotional range was more elastic. As all news is bad news, jowly, dewlapped broadcasters with doleful eyebags drew the fattest pay packets. This was considered important even on the radio.

There were no more letters to the editors of newspapers. There was no Op to the Ed, then no Ed, but newspapers continued to exist. Their pages looked at first as they had under censorship when, instead of the offending article, there appeared a photograph of a donkey. But, after a period of glorious photography, images also departed and the papers reverted to virgin. Oddly, perhaps, the number and page extent of sections remained the same. People still bought their daily at the kiosk; men still slept under them in parks. Traditions were preserved without the clamour of print. It was so much nicer that way.

Not everyone agreed. There were protests, often by unemployed journalists and photographers, but these were mostly silent: we had internalised the impoliteness of noise and were no longer willing to howl slogans. The personal being the political, this extended to domestic life. Fewer violent quarrels were reported. With no way to take things forward, relationships tended to the one-note. Couples who got on badly glared in mutual balefulness; the feelings of those in love were reflected in one another's eyes.

If, at an international level, there was no news, at a local level there was no gossip, so most of us felt better. We ceased to judge people, having no common standards. The first wordless president fought her (his? its? As we could no longer name it, gender scarcely mattered any more) campaign on a quiet platform, gaze fixed on the distant horizon. He (she? it?) knew how to play the new silence. The opposition, opting to fill the space left by speech with random actions, was nowhere. A more liberal, thoughtful community emerged. Or so some of us believed. How could we tell?

Of course there were conspiracy theories. Old folks have always complained that a man's word isn't worth as much as it used to be, that promises nowadays are ten a penny, but radical economists charted a steep devaluation. Once, they proposed, you could have had a conversation word for word, though a picture had always been worth a thousand. That was the system: we knew where we stood, and it was by our words, but the currency went into free fall: a picture to five thousand, ten thousand words, a million! Despite new coinages, soon it was impossible to exchange a word with anyone, unless you traded in the black market of filthy language. And, if you did, there was always the danger you'd be caught on street corners, unable to pay your respects.

Some clung to individual words to fill the gaps as language crumbled but, without sentence structure, they presented as insane, like a homeless man who once lived on the corner of my block and carried round a piece of pipe saying, 'Where's this fit? Where's this fit?' to everyone he met. Except that the word-offerers didn't even form phrases, they just held out each single syllable aggressively, aggrievedly, or hopefully.

As for the rest of us, words still visited sometimes: spork, ostrich, windjammer . . . We wondered where they had come from, what to do with them. Were they a curse or a blessing? We'd pick them up where they dropped, like ravens' bread on soggy ground.

Of course the big brands panicked, employed marketeers to look into whether we had ever had the right words in the first place. Naturally, we never read the results of their research. The new government launched a scheme (no need for secrecy as there's no gossip). Bespoke words were designed along lines dictated by various linguistic systems, and tested. As someone who, until recently, had lived by her words (if there *are* words to live by: as you know, I actually live by the church), I was involved or, perhaps, committed. Under scientific conditions, we exchanged conversations involving satch, ileflower, liisdoktora. We cooed over the new words, nested them, hoping meaning would come and take roost, but meaning never did.

A scattering of the more successful words was put into circulation and, for a while, we tried to popularise them by using them at every opportunity. Despite sponsored 'word placement' in the movies (which were no longer talkies), the new words slipped off the screen: our eyes glazed over. The problem, as it always had been in our country, was one of individualism. By this stage no one expected words to facilitate communication. The experiment resulted not in a common language, but in pockets of parallel neologisms. Being able to name our own things to ourselves gave us comfort. I suspect some people still silently practice this, though of course I cannot tell. I have a feeling their numbers are declining. Even I have stopped. It proved too difficult to keep a bag of words in my head for personal use and to have to reach down into its corners for terms that didn't come out very often. They grew musty. Frankly it was unhygienic.

It was sad to see the last of the signs coming down, but it was also liberating. In the shop that was no longer called COFFEE, you couldn't ask for a coffee any more, but that was OK. You could point, and the coffee tasted better, being only 'that' and not the same thing as everyone else had. It was never the same as the guy behind you's coffee, or the coffee belonging to the guy in front of you. No one had a better cup than you, or a worse. For the first time, whatever it was, was your particular experience and yours alone. The removal of publicly visible words accelerated. Shop windows were smashed, libraries were burned. We may have got carried away. As the number of billboards and street signs dwindled, we realised we had been reading way too much into everything. What did we do with the space in our minds that was constantly processing what we read? Well . . . I guess we processed other things, but what they were, we could no longer say.

Some of us suspected that new things had begun to arrive, things there had never been names for. They caused irritation, as a new word does to an old person, but because there was nothing to call these new things, there was no way to point them out or even to say that they hadn't been there before. People either accommodated them or didn't. We're still not sure whether these things continue to live with us, or if we imagined them all along.

Those people who prefer the new silence are frightened that one day the word will turn. It's a feeling I share, if warily. Words, we had thought, were the opposite of actions but, delving deeper, we found they were also opposed to themselves. Whatever we said, we knew implied its opposite. *It's fine today, I respect you, Will you take out the trash?* ... It had become so difficult to say anything. Our awkwardness got to us. In the republic of words, *I love you* induced anxiety. *How was your day?* would elicit merely a sigh. I think people just got tired, tired of explaining things they'd already said to one another, exhausted by the process of excavating words with words. We were oversensitive perhaps. Do you think we have dumbed ourselves down?

. . .

The last time I saw you we spent days walking around my city. The only voices we heard were foreign: tourists or immigrant workers. You spoke their language but only I could understand the silent natives.

We walked the streets in no direction, following no signs. 'What's that billboard for?' you asked, pointing to the wordless yellow one that was all over town. I told you, 'That's an advert for the billboard company.' You were – temporarily – lost for words. We took photos of the sky disturbed by silent exhalations from the city's rigid gills: air vents linked to air con, to the underground system, but they were all lungs and no voicebox. They couldn't breathe a word. It was cold, so cold I could see my breath next to yours, solid in the frozen air, mingling with the steam of restaurant dinners, of laundries, with warm gusts of metro dust.

The night you left, we went to a shabby pub by the station where we drank bad wine. You talked with the people who worked there: an underclass still allowed to speak because they spoke a different language. They could effect the business we despised, butter us with the courtesies we could no longer practice. Their jobs involved asking for our orders (we would point to the desired item on the illustrated menu), telephoning abroad for crates of imported beer and vodka, telling us to have a nice day. Inside the pub was red as a liver. We worked a little on ours. As we parted we held each other for a little too long and only almost failed to air-kiss.

I am interested in failure, as are we all, because I think it's where we're at. Words failed us a while ago. What will fail us next?

You like women who are quiet? In the end it was not so difficult to let you go: you were only interested in the sound of your own voice. Pretty soon we had nothing left to say to one another. I listened: you looped the same old tape. I tried things that were wordless: I took your hand and pressed it, but feelings meant nothing to you. We were always words apart.

Don't tell me I'm being unreasonable.

Don't talk to me about your girlfriends in the speaking world. Don't repeat the sweet nothings you whisper to them. Don't talk to me about the ones you have yet to meet, who are no doubt wishing aloud for some such coincidence. Don't write back. It is no good calling me: I won't pick up. It's no good texting me, or sending me emails. There's no need to tell me anything. I know it all already. And nothing you could say to me would help.

We're in different places. I'm dead to the word, and you don't have a care in it. You're on top of it: it weighs heavy on my shoulders. So I won't go on. I love you and I'm not aloud, won't allow myself to say it any more. There's no future in it. You wouldn't want a wife who didn't understand you, whose eventual resort could only be dumb insolence – just saying. Love's a word that makes the word go round right enough. It wheels and spins like a coin unsure where to land: heads or tails. Wherever it fell, I would have gone right on to that word's end – for want of a better word – and, like other temporary Miss Words, a better word is what I want *most sincerely*, but I can't say I've ever heard of one.

When I see they're still using words in your country I feel only half-envious, a quarter . . . I also feel a strong swinge (is that even a word?) of embarrassment and pity. Don't be offended: I'm trying to tell it like it is.

You probably think we've all gone quiet over here, that you'll never hear from us again. Yes it is quiet, but we are still thinking. In ways you can no longer describe.

LIKE A FISH NEEDS A . . .

'Always carry a repair outfit.
Take left turns as much as possible.
Never apply your front brake first.'

FLANN O'BRIEN *THE THIRD POLICEMAN*

It's something to do with my cycle. That's what I'll tell the doctor. I'll say I think there's something wrong with my mind. I've read it, about women, didn't want to believe it, but I guess there's some truth in every cliche. Didn't T, who I'd met on a non-date at the Tate, say 'There's a week every month when women go crazy'?

I didn't want to contradict him at the time: I was interested. Yes, I was offended, but, unchallenged, what he'd told me turned over in my mind. He'd arrived on his bike. I'd taken the Tube. The doctor has given me forms to fill. The date led to . . . nothing.

T had a Minotaur physique, spare as the iron seat and handlebars of Picasso's *Bull's Head* (we saw it in a touring exhibition along with Duchamp's readymade bike-wheel, spinning singly in mid-air). I saw T's chest once: two round hard plates with . . . cleavage! A definite gap. That's what you get from all that cycling. I usually go for scholarly types, had never felt anything like it on a man before.

The next time he arrived panting, having cycled up Haverstock Hill to meet me at the Freud Museum. I didn't see his bike. He said he'd parked it round the corner. I showed him mine once. A BSO he called it, a Bike-Shaped Object: looks like a bike, but isn't. 'Suppose I see a bicycle,' said T, quoting philosopher John Searle. 'In such a perceptual situation there is a distinction between the object perceived and the act of perception. If I take away the perception, I am left with a bike; if I take away the bike, I am left with a perception that has no object, for example, a hallucination.'

My bike is far away, in a different city, though I rode it to the station, as I did every day. It's a man's bike. Once I had a woman's cycle but only briefly, in the last months of pregnancy, to triangulate my round scoop of belly. I'm over that now, stepped over it, stepped through. As soon as I stopped bearing, I gave it up, gave it away, can't remember what I did with it. A man's bike – if I can't ride it pregnant, I won't get pregnant. Now there's logic for you.

Many of the objects in the Freud Museum were labelled: quite ordinary objects with extraordinary labels. The violets in the toilets were labelled 'rape', which, in French, is 'viol', and, leant against their pot, a card saying how a mention of the flowers in French had led Freud down a byway into someone's unconscious. Bike words are often French, because of the Tour de France I guess. When someone mentions a bike, said Freud, there must really be a bike, or the idea of a bike, acting on the person's neurones, which are purely physical. Consciousness is physical, and even the idea of a bike is a thing: perception cannot have no object. The violets were displayed in the women's lavatory.

A bicycle is double: two wheels for balance, bipedal, mirrored handlebars, one light in front and one behind, suggesting that wholeness is a co-joined two. But no one kisses in the Freud Museum. No one is coupled. It's a place for groups: schoolkids giggle, earnest friends tour in threes and fives; there are families, even. Only never what makes them.

And, in his study, there's a picture of Freud riding a bicycle. No not riding, but posing with, as though about to leave, and not at the start of a journey – stopped somewhere likely midway. Who are the others he is with? And where, in Hampstead, did Freud park his bike?

. . .

If a fish needs a bicycle, don't drink like one: that's sound advice. If you do, you'll end up outside the station late at night, drunk, cold, fumbling the lock with numb fingers, then, next morning, wrecked, frame stripped down to derailleurs and jockey wheels. It won't be good. For either of you.

Still it's inviting: the bicycle seat, warm negative of a . . . negative. The leather saddle nub's white-stitched ridge, polished and brown, slips neatly between. A good feeling. It can lead you to let go of the brakes. That thing men do that I could never: ride a bike on the level with hands free, hips thrust forward to steer. I've tried, but I don't have the balance, the centre of gravity. This time once again the cogs turned over like bones in their sockets, crunched – dislocated – the gears' vertebrae. When you fall off, get straight back on, they say. But too much freewheeling leads only downhill. It's a vicious cycle.

Next morning I noticed my saddle's leather was split, and from its gash spilled tiny white beads suspended in a sort of gel, white patches on my skirt, brushed absently; more patches, dried, on my inner thighs. Otherwise, trailing my left arm to the elbow, a bacon of road rash – tyre tracks got I don't remember how.

So, ticking the boxes here in the surgery, my bike lashed to a lamp post outside, I'm trying to be more balanced – as to the questions, and also as to the

World-Shaped Object which may exist entirely as I don't perceive it. It seems wrong, despite what I've perceived as correspondent to physical reality, to tick every extreme. It seems wrong not to balance one answer with another, when it might just be an imbalance in my cycle.

Through the doctor's window, set high in the wall as much to exclude thoughts of outside as to shield passers-by from the unwell, I glimpse a man, crouched over a hybrid, with the spine of a rabbit, a *danseur,* dancing on the pedals. It must have been T, cycling away.

EXES

Some people are prolific with xs. Some use a single x, some several small xxxs. Some of them put a number of xs before their names, which are sometimes initials, so that there are more xs than anything else. Some of them put the xs after their names, which are longer than the xs: these people are more likely to use a single x. Some of the xs are unexpected, like the single x from someone who flirted with me, but who withdrew his attentions so that the persistent x seemed insincere, impertinent. Some of them are from people who use too many xxxxxs and oblige me to use too many in return. Most are from friends. Few are from lovers, who tend to drop the xs when they are interested, resume them when they are serious, then drop them again when they no longer feel involved. Only one is from a person whose name is x, whom I slept with once, and who decided not to see me again, which is confusing as I no longer know whether the x is his initial or a term of endearment.

TRAVELLING LIGHT

I am writing in advance of our meeting so you will know the progress of your shipment. Too bulky to carry on the Eurostar, I had it transported to France from London by lorry then ferry in shipping containers. I travelled in the cab of the second truck, encountering no difficulty at French or British customs.

The first container did not arrive in Paris (I'm sure you saw the headlines). When, in the suburb of Ivry-sur-Seine, the second truck, which had given us trouble since Calais, finally broke down, Omar of Bodyshop Carrossier-Quik had the idea of fitting the shipment with wheels. He used industrial castors and welded, rather than drilled, so as not to cause damage. I was able to hire a pickup to tow it to the Gare du Nord where we were mobbed by reporters who were, thankfully, unable to pass the ticket barriers.

On the Paris–Munich train your shipment took up two luggage cars. Difficult to load, as it was all of a piece, I was alarmed to see porters use crowbars, and a circular saw. I protested loudly, but was restrained and was distressed to be unable to prevent its partial dismantling. The container and wheels were discarded, but the inner protective layers remained intact.

In Munich we changed trains without too much difficulty, though there were many papers to complete, and, due to leakage and noise, several fines to pay. I was delayed for two days by these problems. I spent as much time as possible waiting on the platform with the shipment, returning to my hotel only to sleep. We drew stares, some comments, and one (thankfully inconclusive) visit from the transport police. After bribing two railway officials, we were allowed to leave the city by train.

By the time we got to Prague, I could find no one willing to transport it further. I spent most of Tuesday on the pavement outside the station where the shipment had been dumped. It came on to rain and I fretted for the waterproofing so, *faute de mieux*, began to drag it through the streets myself. Without pallet or wheels its base became dirty, the protective cardboard dissolving into rags. As we crossed the Karlovy Bridge pigeons showered upwards, causing crowds to gather, many of whom thought this was an artistic performance so that, when the shipment became stuck between the posts of the bridge's final tower, though I begged them, no one was willing to lend a hand. One man, seeing me in such distress, kindly dislodged it, but wanted to accompany me to my hotel. I was able to put him off because the shipment occupied most of my suite. Its principal part took the bed while I slept between two suitcase stands. How could I go on? The next morning I was able to leave by truck, overpaying a driver from out of town who had not yet heard of the shipment, or of me.

It was possible to reach Belgrade from Budapest only by bus (the rail network, like the shipment, having deteriorated). By now I was able to fit it into a backpack and two suitcases. I crossed Belgrade by tram to the station. Discovering that the train was, again, cancelled, I returned by taxi to the coach stop where I found myself minus a case (the less important one, thank god!). I waited all night at the at the taxi hut where, despite imprecations – tears even – the drivers would not, or could not produce the suitcase. As time was of the essence, and violence promised if I did not leave, I pressed on. On the overnight bus to Sofia, I paid for an extra seat, belted it in beside me, and woke to find it, warm and now only slightly damp, resting against my shoulder. It had loosened and swelled in the southern heat, and gave off a sour smell I found in no way unpleasant, though other passengers moved down the bus. By noon, in the coach's greenhouse atmosphere, it burst its bands, expanded in all directions. Sorry, Sir! Excuse me, Madam! I mewed to it, made chirping noises, coaxed it with thumb and index finger from the floor, the ceiling, chided it into several bags, stuffed excess parts of it into my pockets. While the driver called the police from a service station I said I needed the bathroom and, escaping through a small back window, we evaded arrest.

Running low on money, we hitchhiked from Sofia to Thessaloniki. When they saw what I was carrying, most drivers refused to pick me up but we were given lifts in a removals van and a cattle truck. Between hitches I walked and sometimes ran by the side of the motorway, the larger part of the shipment tied to my back, the rest in two carrier bags. I was grateful for its shade and decreased weight, and only occasionally stopped, sweat dripping from the straps that bit my shoulders, to ask, why me? What gave you the right to award me so heavy, so difficult a burden? I threatened, pleaded – with what? Fate? God? You? No, you're only human, and wasn't I being paid? But never enough! There was no mobile signal. If I had found a payphone I'd have called. Do what you like, you'd have said, as usual. As if I'd any choice. If I'd given up, where would you be and, going on, where would that leave me? Not here . . . Why waste my breath, knowing I would go on? Doesn't everything in the world keep on going?

A labour of love, then? And what better than to be allowed to experience love, whatever its price?

On the train from Thessaloniki to Athens, I cradled it in my lap, wrapped in my scarf, rocking with the swaying train. We had been through so much together. Fellow passengers mistook it for a baby, or a dog.

I took a bus from Athens station, what remained of the shipment in a single bag. Alighting at Monastiraki I was the victim of a purse-snatcher but fought back, losing the bag but retaining more than half of its contents.

I reached the hotel with no more than crumbs. There must have been a hole in my pocket. I traced and retraced my steps but the ground was yellow as cake; birds might have taken what was scattered. Here is what's left, in one of the hotel's ashtrays. I will keep watch over it until you join me. My eyes will not leave it for a moment.

You will find me in the roof bar of the Attalos Hotel, where I await your arrival, and that of your return shipment.

Yours etc.

FEMME MAISON

You wanted to look different for him. You wanted a change of a dress. You wanted a new dress you had never seen before. You wanted to be someone else, someone neither of you knew.

But then you have not met Him yet.

He will take you away from all this. As things are, you can't go on in any way: everything is missing. If you were somewhere else, you would already be wearing the different dress, a summer dress. You would be comfortable. But the dress you have is too big. You can't wear your dress if you can't alter it, and you don't have sewing-machine needles. You broke the last one and the shop didn't have any more.

You were typing on your laptop: something important, you can't remember, but you began to search for sewing-machine needles.

It's the same all over the house. You go to look for things but they are always in the wrong room. Where are they? They might have been left outside in the rain. They might have been put on a high shelf so the children would not get them.

No sooner is there something to do than it requires something else to do it with. The piece of information needed is always at one remove: scribbled on an envelope already in the recycling; printed on an old bank statement, perhaps shredded; written in a letter filed in the cabinet you don't open any more.

It's a question of systems. Go upstairs and you'll notice a tea towel that should be in the kitchen. Bring it down and there are the books that should be by your bed. How did they change places? Why didn't you notice the books before you went upstairs for the tea towel? Then you could have taken them up and put them by the bed and picked up the tea towel and taken it down. Except it wasn't the tea towel you went to look for, was it? It was something else, but exactly what you can't remember.

Sewing-machine needles.

You should have established some kind of process.

There *is* a process to the day. You eat at established times though it's such a bother to make. Always afterwards you find a wrapper without a name snaking across the kitchen surface. What is it from? If it is vacant, why was it not cleared? How did you miss it? On tables small things migrate according to the season: the seals from plastic milk cartons, beer bottle lids (though it was He who drank beer whereas you drink wine). How did they get there? Why were they not removed? There must be a way to get rid of them.

You forget to wash your hands before reopening your laptop. Its keys are slick with butter. Not with jam, at least, but this is because the jam is still in the shop where you forgot to buy it. You came away with 250g of cherries and a pint of milk. The milk you needed, undoubtedly. You needed cocoa but they did not have cocoa. The queue was long and you were distracted by the labels of the wine bottles behind the counter, not the bottles with graphics and fancy typography but the bottles with pictures of chateaux, sea bays, farmhouses. You walked into each of these landscapes as if you were visiting. If you were in those places, any of those places, you could wear the dress instead of tight urban jeans, the dress that needs altering. You could have been comfortable.

You go into the post office in case there is something else you need. Each time you go in you look at the magazines and consider buying *Vogue*. You do not buy it. Next time you shop you will do the same thing.

All your life you've been asked to choose: to be the woman who didn't drink canned sodas, who didn't watch American television programmes, who would never, even in fun, decorate her home with Anaglypta wallpaper. Some of these injunctions you have overturned, but there are always fresh ones. You choose not to choose any more.

It's not only your fault. After the children left, bit by bit you and He abandoned the house, eating takeaways, spending evenings in cafes. At one point you could afford to eat out every weekend. But the house missed you. The fresh flowers you bought were, it knew, an insult, a sop. That's why you knew He had to go.

But how did your keyboard get so dirty? The dust builds all over the house, always on a different surface. You chase it with a corner of the dress's sleeve. The dirt is still there, grey and furry. It has merely transferred. You are now part of it.

After He was gone, things altered. You expanded into the areas of the house you hadn't previously used: the study, the front room. You felt, for the first time, that they were yours. You also felt you owed it to them.

But the house is still not a perfect fit. Still things surprise you. When you try to get to the cupboard holding the dusters, there is something in the way: a stand of washing, a tall stool from the counter. Who put them there?

You turn, you remember – the laptop. You had forgotten. You remember. You had got up. You had wanted to clean the keyboard. You had gone to find a duster.

Something was altered. What was it?

Wait. You remember.

You had cut but you had not pasted.

Your words hover in vacant space. You turn. You run. You will save them. You paste. They are still there.

How could you have left them? How could you have forgotten? How did you manage to leave your thought at its waist to search for the duster? How did you fail to get the duster but return to the laptop?

What you had written might have been lost forever. The words are still there. But so is the dust.

You thought it would be OK after He was gone. You thought you'd have more time for work, for fussless-ness. But the house is relentless.

The fridge must occasionally be defrosted. Something knocks in the icebox. Frost has grown on the walls of the cool section as moss does on a tomb but inverse, its fingers reaching down towards the salad drawer. An afternoon hacking though the ice forest may reach a single embryonically suspended fish finger.

You still attempt to generate one bag of rubbish each week: the bin demands it. The dishwasher is completely redundant. The washing machine begs to be used but your piles of laundry are dwindling, pathetic. They barely skim the bottom of the drum: they are hardly dirty.

Vines slap against the window. On the patio the barbecue is rotting, the lawnmower is rusting. How are you meant to attack the overgrowing jasmine? With the blunted shears? With the kitchen scissors?

Some things used to matter so much: the exact shade of green of the garden chairs, which did not match the exact shade of green of the garden table. Now both are sun-bleached, flaking. 'A Generous Family House.' That's what the estate agent said when he came to value it, 'Generous.' For a few weeks he sent you emails: would you sell? But that was years ago.

The machines wait patiently. They must wait. In the daily round, certain chairs must be sat in.

You put the dress into the washing machine. It will be clean before it is altered. You add detergent, switch it on. The drum goes round and round. The dress is not dirty but perhaps dusty. The dust travels from the dress to the inside of the washing machine, then out through the tubes. The house senses an exchange. It is satisfied.

DUNNET

In the past tense, it was a bird.

Whodunnit didn't matter, whether it was *I, said the sparrow*, or the snowy, or the barn – hoo-ever. Who would lay the blame on top of each other like that hand-slapping game for two? There's never a winner. Pull the bottom one out – the whole thing beetles over.

By the cliff's edge, I'd not thought to find a dunnock, a sparrow, like, with those markings. It was way out of its neck of the woods. Seabirds live on cliffs in vertical colonies without the hazards of horizontal pairing. It might have been one of them that did for it. The country code says 'cliffs have inherent dangers,' but that's a horse of a different feather. When I picked it up, its neck flopped back. It was only recently dead.

I didn't know the name till after, but that was where we were, outside Dunnet, a village in Scotland with its Mary-Ann's Cottage Preserved Croft, its C H Haygarth & Sons Scotland's Oldest Practising Gunmakers, its family-run hotel with twelve bedrooms and two bars, its church whose history dates from 1280 – but like I said, who's counting?

When something's gone it's gone. I'm only winging it through here.

All writers are itinerary. And all books look the same in the dark.

TWO SECRETARIES

We are two secretaries. We sit in the lower ground floor office where there is little light. It is an old building, but it lends the business class so we do not mind about the dark.

That is where the description of us as a pair ends. If you come into the building you will see two secretaries, one of which is me. We may look alike, but we are not. K is the other secretary. That is, she is a secretary: I am a clerical assistant. I have asked to be called a clerical assistant, so that is what people call me. They can see that I am not a secretary. I am not trained in secretarial skills, though I can type and also take shorthand. I am a recent graduate. I have a degree. I do not expect to stop here for long. K has been a secretary for a number of years. She is, no doubt, a good secretary and, no doubt, wants to be a secretary all her life, although sometimes she likes to call herself an office manager.

I am good at my job. It doesn't take much to be a secretary. For instance, L, one of the department assistants, wanted some paper clips for her department from office supplies. She requested coloured paper clips but I ordered plain. I had been asked to keep costs down and this was something I did voluntarily. I showed my initiative. I was surprised when L wasn't pleased but I'm sure those higher up in her department appreciated it. I try to go to lunch with the assistants in the offices, sometimes even with the juniors. This is because someday soon I will be working with them, especially those high enough up to appreciate my initiative.

K wears a blue skirt suit with a jacket just the same colour. She wears it every day. Her hair is permed. She wears sheer hosiery. She has a boyfriend. One day she confided in me that she wants to marry him but she is not so sure he wants to marry her. They are moving in together, to an apartment in a suburb. They cannot agree on the paint colours for the walls. She likes lilac, he likes primrose.

I would not paint my walls either lilac or primrose. When I move in with a boyfriend, which is something that, like an apartment, I will also have someday, we will not live in a suburb but in the centre of town. Like the office our flat will be in an old building. It will have class. Right now I live in an outer suburb. My lease is up soon, and my flatmates are finding somewhere new. I have plans to find somewhere new too, but not with them, and much nearer the centre. Because I also have plans, I can sympathise with K's plans without letting her know I don't like primrose or lilac, or the suburbs. I can be happy for her and I can hope she gets what she wants, which is not at all what I would want.

K ordered a new office machine. It was put beside my desk. As its wrapping was removed the smell of plastic hit the whole office. It is an old-fashioned office: the machine is the only modern thing in it. It is pearl grey: a whale of a thing. K switched it on and it started to whirr. I began to cough quite loudly like this: 'eheugh, eheugh!' These were real coughs but I made them even louder to show how bad the smell was. The smell the machine produced was so different to everything else in the building, which is made of paper and wood, that it made me feel sick, and so I went and stood in the hall to breathe the fresh air. K said, *how long are you going to keep on doing that?* And I said, *Until the smell goes away. I will come back every time I have to answer the phone* (this is one of my duties). K said nothing.

One lunchtime all the assistants invited me to have lunch with them. I was surprised and pleased. They said they knew that K was being unpleasant to me about my housing situation and that I had cried and that they were sorry. I was surprised because I hadn't noticed that K was being at all unpleasant. However I didn't say anything as I was pleased to be out with the assistants and to know where they lunched. The next day I hoped to have lunch with the assistants again but it seems they do not always go out for lunch together. This is a pity because lunch is one of the things I am looking forward to as soon as I get to assistant level.

K and I don't speak much now. Sometimes K asks me a polite question about my housing situation and sometimes I ask K a polite question about her boyfriend.

K has ordered a large green fabric screen from office supplies. This is despite our being asked to keep costs down. She has put the screen in front of her so that she sits between the screen and the window. I get less light. When K's phone rings I don't answer it. It is behind her screen and everything that goes on behind her screen is her own business. And when my phone rings K doesn't answer it. But this is all OK as in any case I do not expect to stop here for very long.

ENZO PONZA

I was still quite a small girl when I decided to kidnap Enzo Ponza.

I remember clearly deciding it would be him. He was standing in one of the sloping streets of shabby residential buildings that lead down to the harbour off the main road. Who knows if he lived there? He was speaking to someone who got into a car with a small child, perhaps belonging to one of them, or the other. When they drove away, he came quietly, and at once, almost as though expecting it.

I had never seen him before.

I led him to our block and up the fire escape. When we got to my floor we sat at the table on the balcony that is accessed from the walkway. I did not yet want to take him inside the flat. He sat facing in, I facing out, in case I saw anyone coming to rescue him. He was wearing a long black coat, and had long black moustaches. He looked sad, not angry, or maybe just the kind of sad some adults have on their faces all the time. I guess they call it melancholy. He did not look me in the eye. He said nothing.

I brought food out to him and he ate, uncomplaining. My parents, indoors, saw him through the window but made no comment. That night they suffered him to lie down on the settee, fully clothed. They asked no questions. Nor did he. He made no attempt to leave.

I can't say exactly when he began permanently to live in our flat. He was accommodating, waiting until everyone had gone to bed to unfold a mattress in the living room, which he stowed away before breakfast. I think sometimes he even slept in the hall. My mother fed him without protest. My father shared his newspaper in silence. Enzo Ponza spent most of his time sitting: at the table, where he played patience; on the settee, where he watched television. He seemed to enjoy the football most, but never demanded a change of channel. No one liked to sit next to Enzo Ponza, but no one asked him to move. To challenge him would have been to acknowledge his existence. No one complained about his use of the bathroom early in the morning while we all got ready for school or work. No one complained that he left squeezed teabags bleeding by the sink. His disposition was taciturn. Though my parents occasionally addressed him on practical matters – 'pass the salt,' or 'move your feet so I can hoover' – my younger siblings never mentioned him at all. Perhaps they thought he always had been there.

In the early days, he never removed his coat. I have no idea what he did while I was at school, while my parents were at work. I did not ask him as he seemed preoccupied, as preoccupied with the mysteries of his own adulthood as my mother and father were with theirs. When we returned, there he was, sitting on the settee, sometimes smoking – something neither of my parents did – sometimes reading the newspaper, his feet up, one sock off so he could rub between his toes. While I did my homework, he sat opposite me at the table, reading the western novels that had belonged to my grandfather. He never once asked when I would let him go.

For the first few years, he never went out. He cut his hair and his moustaches himself with our nail scissors. We would sometimes find the trimmings in the sink. He must have washed his single set of clothes while we were at school, at work, sitting naked while they dried. We never discovered his underwear dripping on the lines strung over the bath.

If we came home to find him, say, frying eggs in the kitchen, he became particularly reserved, would act like he had been discovered at something illegal which, I suppose, they being technically our eggs, he had. The situation was complex as, ostensibly, he was here against his will, so we had no avenue for complaint. During that time, these abruptly finished activities were all we could discover of his inner life.

It was not until some years later that I began to encourage him to go outside. I had reached my teens and, with expanded horizons, felt a new sense of responsibility. Enzo Ponza was mine, after all; my parents didn't interfere any more than they had with the goldfish, or the guinea pig. They had been hands-off in these matters: if I did something wrong, the consequences, and the lesson, would be mine. Perhaps they felt the same in this case. I became concerned for Enzo Ponza's health, and began, each day, to lead him into the green area between the flats, and encourage him to walk about, to do stretching exercises, and pull-ups on the children's climbing frame.

Over the years, my parents began occasionally to acknowledge his presence. My mother, catching Enzo Ponza's evaluating glances in the hall mirror, began to seek his approval on her choice of clothing. If he nodded, she would go out to work, satisfied with her appearance, if not, she would go back and change. She started to invite her friends in more often, perhaps with the idea of matchmaking, though this subject was never mentioned. They would sit round the small collapsible card table and play canasta, in which Enzo Ponza did not join. He said little. He was a good listener and the women liked him, though none of them seemed to want to take things further. Sometimes he walked with one of them in the green bit between the flats, but I don't think these walks were ever romantic. I think the women confided in him – and some, perhaps in return, contributed to his supply of cigarettes, whose sources remained mysterious – but he never relayed what they said.

My parents asked him to contribute neither to the housework nor expenses, but treated him as a perpetual guest. However, they found some uses for him. They occasionally asked him to babysit so they could go out, which they, nevertheless, did infrequently, having no real wish to. Poverty was enough to save us from our desires. We did not drink or love casually, knowing we'd have to get up early the morning after, and that any consequences could be long-term.

Be careful what you take on, my father said. I knew what he was talking about. The threat of tomorrow made me timid as they were. I think this is why my parents began to send Enzo Ponza along when I went on dates with boys from school. My romantic activities were constrained, it's true, but I understood my responsibilities. My social life restricted, I passed my exams with good marks but didn't go on to college, not wanting to incur a loan. Instead I took a shorthand class, and began to work in the office of the local newspaper, in the library, which was, then, still microfiche and clippings held in sliding shelves of brown hanging files.

I married a man I met at work (the only place I was free from my parents, and Mr Ponza). He worked in the production department and, during the early years of our relationship, his fingers were always inky. We had three children, a boy, then boy-and-girl twins, before our marriage dissolved and I returned with my children, and Enzo Ponza, to my parents' flat. My other siblings were long gone, and, as my father – though always a non-smoker – had died from lung cancer, my mother was, perhaps, glad enough to have us, though at her advanced age she was so self-absorbed it was difficult to tell. We kept the flat clean and in good repair, cooked for her, and I was able to shoulder the household expenses. Because of my special knowledge of the newspaper archive I had been able to get my old job back, overseeing its digitisation, the completion of which, I suspected, might make me finally redundant. Enzo Ponza, as always, seldom left the flat but busied himself unobtrusively about household tasks. We did not discuss this arrangement, but found it worked to everyone's satisfaction. My mother seemed particularly to enjoy EP's company and, sometimes, I thought that she recognised him from the old days, though neither of them said a word.

It was some time after my return to the library that I was asked to investigate press clippings regarding Enzo Ponza. A member of the public called, anonymously enquiring about material relating to Enzo Ponza's fear of snakes. I found nothing in the recently digitised archive, and was reluctant to go back to the older hanging files, whose metal frames bit my fingers each time my hands ventured between them. Nevertheless I searched under both E and P, finally finding a crumpled clipping with a blurry picture and an article beneath. Could that be my Enzo? Who could tell. The man had been photographed from above, his face in shadow. It was not a willing photo. He did not have the current Enzo's bald patch, but that could have been no more than a matter of time.

Beneath the photo, the caption: NOTORIOUS PONZA: I HIT OUT BECAUSE I FEARED I WOULD BE STABBED.

Mr Ponza stood accused of something I will not relate here.

When I returned home that night, Enzo Ponza had put my children to bed. They were sleeping calmly. He had eaten the salad I had prepared for him before I left for work, and was sitting at the card table, smoking and looking at the newspaper, sometimes reading, sometimes staring out of the window. Was he this same Enzo Ponza, who was surely still in prison, though the piece had said 'charged' but not 'convicted'. I thought about asking him, but the time did not seem right.

His moustache is white now, as is his hair, which he wears longer than he used to, its wings scraped back into a ponytail that circles the bald patch that has become a dome. His teeth are yellow with nicotine, and nibbed round the edges with brown. His shoulders are rounded and there is a single crease of fat across the back of his neck. He is now relaxed enough in the flat to take off his shirt in hot weather, and to sit at the card table wearing nothing but a singlet and pants. How intimately I know him, and yet how little. His demands, like those of my children, are small, inarticulate, made only through expectation. I am happy to meet them.

I sometimes wonder about our meeting. Why should a small girl have chosen, of all people, such a distasteful ruin of the masculine, all open pores, sweat stains and tobacco filaments – and someone of whose circumstances she knew nothing? The evenings of this last summer we sat at the balcony table, him opposite me, facing toward the flat, as always, caring nothing for the view.

I asked him, once, the question to which I wanted an answer. He waved a cigarette, which he had brought from his breast pocket, and lighting it, said, 'You know how it is . . .' Of course I didn't. I never asked him again.

What has he spared me, this Enzo Ponza? What, with his constant presence, has he prevented happening in my life, and what, if anything, has he caused to happen? Does he care for me, my mother, my children? Is he escaping something, or is he just biding his time? Why, when I invited him into my life, did he agree to stay? And why did I never investigate whether he had any living relatives to whom I could send a ransom note?

Perhaps only I understood his value. How many people offer themselves so simply? At our age? At any age? Not many.

Kidnapping Enzo Ponza was my one act of love, and maybe it was his too.

THE SUITCASE DOG

(For the first Ben.)

'Pets up to 25 lbs are allowed to check into your room with you and stay by your side.'

THE ACE HOTEL

I am the suitcase dog. My head fits through a hole. I am portable.

My jaws snap shut on hinges. In the hotel there is no postman. In the hotel there is no letterbox. My jaws snap shut on nothing. What I defend is not my territory.

Objects, Food, Rooms. My life goes up and down. In the service elevator I am descended. I walk through the front door. I walk through the back door onto the cobbles where the kitcheners smoke where strange smells are renewed daily. I may not pee on the carpet. I may not pee in the flowerpot.

I am walked up and down the corridor. I am walked up and down the lobby. I am walked up. I am walked down.

I am walked but, also, I am walking.

Wait.

What if I walked without being walked. Where would I (who would I) walk?

I slip the leash.

I go howling down the long red tongue, hear something, chase nothing. It still goes. I stop. I find myself at a loss.

And I am lost.

I am shut out of something. I position myself, as always, in front of a door, but now on the outside, which is the wrong way round – or I am. In any case, no one comes when I whine. No one comes when I scratch. So I walk.

I walk on things that hear me differently: something hard on which each nail hits separately till I am twenty dogs – then something soft (I disappear). I listen for the way. Somewhere else a cleaner hums. I hear the carpet fibres pulled upright.

Then I try down and, after so many downs, I go sit in a bush in this indoor landscape. It is like the places I have waited before, but the earth beneath it is not brown. Still, all substances are like earth. All can be dug through – blanket, chair, floor – to find the centre. And there is a centre to everything; I am sure of that.

It tinkles, the water on glass in the little arrangement in which I sit. And there are people. So I am somewhere. In a dining room? That is what this hush is: chatter.

Legs pass – not the right legs, I care for no above-the-knee – for a long time. Until.

I am frightened. Really, what isn't?

Wait.

This one isn't.

I will bite the diners' heads off!

There is nothing so little, so little because I am nothing little, not here, not so little as you would think, eh?

By which time I am on a plate, not sure if I am pet or meat, or altogether meat on the outside, meat on the inside. But. (Bark!) Be less timid, please. Don't be upset. (Wags.)

However.

A dog is not a nail of any kind, and I can be removed, taken to lost property, four-wheeled, at my back a pull-out handle, until my owner claims me, wheels me. I am walked. Up, and down. After which I am kept in.

I stay here behind the door, lying where light is not across. It crosses, does not stay. It shadows. What kind of substance is a hotel? Sometimes I break it apart to find out, always different bits. Anything not torn is for me. I am what's waiting for it. But inside there is no satisfaction, only something white that puffs. It is not food. I lie. I watch what has four legs, carefully. I have four legs and a broad back, just the same. It does not move, though it also bears things.

I watch it all afternoon.

It says:

Anyone remember your first puberty? Anyone? Remember.

I was snipped. I do not desire other dogs but to repel them. I am always desiring something. Everything here isn't dog. No more am I, oh no, not any more. I am baggage, picked up with the suitcases, travelled in the elevator, taken out between the hotel's revolving doors. In any case, I am already carried away.

I am the world's inconvenience. Except my own.

THE STORY OF OUR NATION

Tomorrow morning I will get up and again begin work on the story of our nation.

The story of our nation will be heroic. It will also be domestic spectacular pathetic operatic comic tragic tragicomic. The story of our nation will have acrobatics close-ups magic tricks panning shots kabuki marching bands and ice dancing. There will be Gorgeous and Realistic Scenery, an Original Soundtrack, Reflex and Precision-Based Combat with Manual Blocking and Dodging. There will be Tons of Enemy Types including Huge Prehistoric Creatures. There will be Item Enhancement. There will be First-Person Mode, as well as many other Modes. There will be drinks and ices at the intervals (of which there will be several).

In fact the story of our nation will involve everything. But, as yet, we are only at the research stage. At present I am working on hedgerows. It is a delicate job, and painstaking. I count the leaves and measure each.

In spring, new leaves appear and must be categorised differently – by colour and dimension in their pale and unfurled state – to the same leaves as they manifest in full green, and to the tough dark leaves they become in September, amongst the hawthorn berries. So that objects in the world will now load in more smoothly, each morning I make an early start. The weather this month is mild and, like most clients (for we, being of this nation, are clients too), I take breakfast to work. There is a stop for coffee at 11am, and at 1pm lunch in the field kitchen. The atmosphere is jolly. There is camaraderie. We are comrades. Because of improvements, inviting other characters into a large group in a different zone will no longer cause desynching issues. Or perhaps it's just the season, or the knowledge we are doing something good, in it together, one nation under the groove.

Some days I start even earlier. I'm not the only one. Walking before dawn I can't see the people, just dark shapes passing dark houses – only the landing lights on – in a silage of cheap perfume. Albanian voices, Polish voices: they're the ones who'll work 'unsocial hours', which must be recorded just the same as daylight ones, though, having newly arrived in the country, some of them do it for sheer love. As do I. I use weekends to catch up. I like the mornings best.

I wake early, drink coffee, revise the week's work, though while I am working I am distracted by recording what happens those mornings. They're so good, I wouldn't want to lose them. The nation wouldn't want to lose them.

My job is a good one. The hedge fund ensures fair pay and conditions. Even when it rains, the rate and size of drops doesn't bother me; I am not in the water department. I am one of the lucky ones: others count the cracks in concrete, monitor bad air levels at junctions, size up the marble chips in industrial flooring. Still others measure shadows, clock them to time, test their density, calibrate the light that arcs night ceilings through the slits between curtains, the slats of blinds: light from cars, from street lamps. Some measure the gaps between doors and doorsills, the colour spectrum of hair on cutting-room floors. Somebody has to do it. Negative or positive, mass observation is observation of mass and, though this will be our nation's story, it will not be fiction: we have to keep it real. Strictly.

We had books, of course, before, and magazines. We had movies, we had TV shows, also the internet. There, stories were parallel but not the real thing. What was missing was bare fact. So we were taken from jobs at KFC, the BMA, the IMF, the AA, MSN (and HP), the RAC, the RAF, and TGI Fridays, from work in

HE, HR, PR, IT; on PhDs, on MBAs, on GCSEs, from departments handling production and distribution. There was enough stuff already. We had it all: white goods, brown goods, green belts, grey areas, thin blue lines, yellow perils, red mists, you name it. We knew in our hearts it was time to stop making any more. It was time to sit back and look at what we'd got.

. . .

After work, in the evenings, our results are shown on TV. I watch nature programmes, mostly, as that's my field: the volume of water in our national rivers, the collective weight of the nation's sheep, the mean hue of the pink part of daisies, broken down by region. I also have a side project (such hobbies are encouraged). Each night I count the hairs on my head. The result is sometimes even (oddly, perhaps, more often odd). I record the results in my personal log. My height and weight are noted each morning. I will not be forgotten. When asked for my papers I will present them: the list of diet shakes in my cupboard, the sell-by date of each packet in my fridge, the three sizes of my various shoes, the density of my earlobes in mass per unit volume, everything correctly categorised. I ensure (for instance) that my food is no longer listed in several places in the filters, that it shows up only under Consumables, that my fruit bowl, where the avocados sulk like slugs, is in a category distinct from the flies that crawl upside down on my skylight (I know their trajectories, the hours of their deaths). I shall wait for approval without fear: nothing will be missing. Everything about me will be remembered.

You know, the only thing I can't bear is, we all change. Like, I used to have a fairly irresponsible job – thorns, if you must know – and there were certain things I wouldn't say to anyone, wouldn't think of saying. But, now I'm in hedges, I've grown, blossomed, and there are things I'll say quite casually, sometimes involving cussing even (but in a friendly way, naturally), knowing that my words will be received in a friendly way, even the cuss ones, though I know they wouldn't have been before. And now I know they might even be received in a friendly way by people who don't know I have the job I have, because I have things that job has brought me, like confidence and a certain degree of social ease. And when I meet some of those people who knew me from before, they double-take, not because I'm doing the job I'm doing now, but because I'm doing it with comfort, as though I'd always done it. I want to tell them, I didn't mean to change.

I don't intend to change any more.

I live alone. It's been that way for a while, and I think it will continue. More change would be too much to calculate. *How long is forever? How deep is your love?* What scale, what increments would I use? What chance would I have with anyone else when I still know so little of myself? It is necessary that such encounters have improved stability. More must be recorded if I am – if we are – to count for anything. After all, *To know you is to love you* . . . or is it, *To love someone else you have to love yourself*? Or maybe it's just, *know thyself*? Though with that *thy* I stop thinking of myself immediately, and instead think about who would use such a word, and wonder if they're in some play.

The story of our nation will not be like some play. Once all the data is inputted there will be scenes you can no longer walk away from, scenes in which you will no longer revive. That's as it should be. There will, equally and oppositely, be scenarios in which it is possible. This will prevent you from getting your quest into an uncompletable state. Completion is only a matter of time, and time is a One-Time Redeemable Item. To give it to another character, you must deposit it in your shared inventory, accessed from major cities. To delete a character when this Item is in the inventory means it could be permanently lost.

In the story of our nation nothing will be lost. The story of our nation will be entirely true, and it will be a good story, despite its being true. Whatever we find the truth to be, it is impossible that it should be otherwise than good. It will be better than history, updated and analysed each moment for everyone to view. Though not synonymous with, it will be identical to the truth: once we input all the figures you will be able to see everything in a flash and, at the same time, there will be overviews, there will be breakdowns, there will be footnotes, and there will be headlines so that everyone will be able to comprehend the greatness of our nation which will be suddenly cohesive, like one of those ads that shows all the races mixing then the camera pulls out so they form the giant letters of a single word, not even a word, something more instant, conveying feeling as well as meaning – a logo, perhaps.

When it is all done, what shall we do? Or – no – there is no reason to think about that: it will never be done, it will always be doing. Once we reach a certain level, it will continue to do, even as we watch ourselves doing it. And that's the joy in it, though always to be thinking about the story – which is to always be thinking about thinking about the story – will become such a tremendous effort that it will be difficult ever to be light about it, which, sometimes, is what the story of our nation most requires. How wonderful it would be to stop thinking, or rather, to pause from thinking, to turn the story inside out like a glove, and lay it seamy side out, if only for an instant. How painstaking, what delicate work. But, look! There. It's done, and with hardly any effort either (except that the two types of gloves I have are (1) sheepskin 'driving' gloves, that I do not use for driving, but which nevertheless have ridges of external decorative stitching, and (2) rubber gloves, which have no seams at all). Whatever. The story of our nation needs these sudden turns, I could say *volte-face*(s?), but I might be straying beyond our national remit.

Being on the inside (as everyone is) I could cheat – one leaf's as good as another – but I've only occasionally been tempted to fiddle the figures. No, not when the girls in Information check my stats against the pale bulk of my body, but to fix issues, as when performing a new filter the page is reset to page 0, or where the map will not zoom properly, or to clarify tooltips so they better reflect the correct key presses after rebinding the associated keys. I've never given in to these temptations. My job – our job – is only to observe. Even to measure is to move, which implies, also: to disturb the dust, to make waves. To minimise this we have been issued with rubber gloves, with wellingtons, with waterproof trousers, with mudguards, with condoms. We have been issued with hairnets, fishnets, falsies, gas masks, hygienic paper toilet seat covers, cling film. We will change nothing, not even by being there.

The motorways lie quiet.

Nothing new is made.

Only nature we cannot stop. And thought, if that's a thing.

Changes of season are the most difficult. Yesterday the spiders appeared (where do they come from?). Just past midsummer they lay trails from branch to branch suspending shields visible only by their live centres. These spiders are brown and stripy. The spiders that come later are black. I do not remember them coming this early before. Is this anomaly or just memoryfail?

In the fields behind the hedge I am presently working on, I can see people stooping to furrows with calibrators and rulers. The scent of hedge-roses has reached it highest concentration of ouE, but I have no need to worry. It's being covered. A SWAT team has been flown in to work on the spiders. They are videoed audioed tasted pinched analysed.

I type results into my handheld. As they are numbers on a screen, there is room for many more, as many as there are leaves on a tree.

One day, when I have finished with hedges, I will turn my attention to horse chestnuts.

BLUE

I am on holiday in a house with no mirrors.

My friend is here with me. She has agreed to share the house I have rented for the summer.

I see my friend in her swimsuit. She has good legs, very good legs. I can see them but I cannot see my own legs. If I want to see my own legs I must stand on the chair in the dark dining room and look at them reflected in the glass of the dark picture above the mantelpiece. Even attached to no one I know they are my legs and I know they are not so good as my friend's.

The house is furnished with the dirt-ring of its owners' lives. Some of it is very good, some of it is very bad, but nothing is perfect. The chairs' legs are curved and polished, but they are chipped. The curved handles of the teacups are chipped, but they have gold rims, which are worn. The bathroom cabinet is made of chipboard. Its legs are missing. It has only plastic and metal stumps.

The decor of the house is blue, which I do not like. My friend is reading a book I do not like. Though I have not read it, I know it is not a good book. This makes things more even.

The bottom of the swimming pool outside the house is painted blue. The sky is blue, unclouded. The grass is blue in the strong sun. I pull a long string of skin, like dried grass, from a scratch on my shin. My friend jumps into the pool, her good legs flow behind her like contrails.

I read my book.

SIMPLE HANS

This morning I had my first-ever cup of coffee. It was a very tiny cup, and made me feel like a giant. We were in a coffee shop. He was much younger than me. I knew that, but he didn't. He was a grown-up, but a very new one. I have spent a very long time as a young child, much longer than most. I dyed my hair for the occasion, but the chin hairs were already growing on me. They were sharp and tough as pig bristles. He was nervous. He told me about something called the internet. I pretended I knew all about it already.

When we went to bed, his limbs were white and speckled. They had too many angles. His cock was a right-angle to mine. There seemed too many of them, always going in and out of something else. Outside the cafe, an old friend of my father's had seen me walking with him, and had shouted, 'Cradle snatcher!' We pretended she was trying to communicate with someone else.

After that we spoke by instant message. He sent me 'Who knew cheese exploded?!?!?'

I tried to send him a guinea pig, but it wouldn't go through the screen, though I pushed and pushed.

He wasn't there. The guinea pig remained with me. I tried to put my cock in the screen. It didn't work. It hardly mattered. After the guinea pig, the pale guy didn't want to see me again.

I tried other things: Grindr, Tinder, OkCupid, but they were all the same. There seemed to be no communication in the world, so I left the town where I was born, as all youngest sons should. It was time for me to go and seek my fortune.

I rented a bedsit in a suburb of a small seaside town. After a week in this new place no fortune arrived. It was winter. The sun slanted quick and narrow across the day. Dark came too soon and I slept. There was not enough daylight for a fortune to appear.

In the meantime I liked to look at the ads in corner-shop windows, which made me feel part of this new place, and also allowed me a frisson of contempt for the sellers of second-hand children's clothes, and *Ironing Services*, and *Bums 'n Tums for Mums*. This is not nice but it's OK: I am not from here and, being lucky, don't have to worry about such things. I saw Helen's ad in the shop window. On a small card it said, *Victorias*

Secret Massages for the Discerning. I thought, I'd have put a semicolon, or a colon. There wasn't even a full stop. Or an apostrophe. Of course she wasn't called Victoria.

I booked an appointment on the phone. 'What name?' said Helen, who, I had thought, was called Victoria. I said my name. 'You don't want to give your name?' said Helen. 'That's OK.' 'That is my name,' I said. 'Yes,' said Helen, 'I know.'

Helen lived in a flat above another shop in the same high street. It sold electrical goods. Or maybe the flat was where she worked. I sat in a room that might have been a waiting room or might have been a living room. There was a floral sofa. She shouldn't have bought such a pale print. No, it was a waiting room, not a front room; there was no direction anywhere, not towards a telly, or a fireplace, or a window. Everything faced in, the chairs not quite towards each other. They nudged each other's corners, tried not to notice. I stared at a patch of wall under a shelf made of stick-on wood-effect vinyl with a pot plant on it.

Helen was wearing a white uniform like a nurse. I could see what she was wearing underneath, like a comedy nurse, not a real healthcare official. When I took the pale boy to A&E the nurses wore garments like grocery plastic bags in pastel blues and greens, gathered around their wrists and ankles with elastic.

They wore jellyfish on their heads, which were also in marine colours. You couldn't tell if they were boy or girl.

Helen said, 'Normally there's me or Isa, but today there's just me. Isa's here on Saturdays, Sundays, and Tuesday afternoons. If you want Isa you'll have to book one of those slots. I'm here all the time.' She said, 'How old are you?' She said, 'It's adults only. And usually men.' I said, 'I'm not a woman, you know, and I'm not as young as I look.'

She took me next door and I stripped and lay on a hospital gurney on a fresh white towel.

When she had massaged me for a while, I pulled her towards me and she said that wasn't in the deal. She said I'd have to pay extra but frankly no one ever wanted extras – this was a stingy town. And unimaginative: think of all the churches. This is the part in the story when it's normal for youngest sons to resist, or perhaps to give in: I can't remember. Her cunt was dry and unused, having never been part of a deal, ever. I stuck my head between her legs and rubbed my hair into hers causing static electricity. She opened like an oyster bread-bun lips forced apart by a whorl of stiff whipped cream – you can buy them in Greggs Bakery on the high street. It tasted of salt and air, just the same as the cream. They say the sea air's good for you. Or perhaps she had the window open. A little knob of flesh stood out at the top of her cunt. I wanted to bite it, but she pulled back as my teeth snapped closed.

I came again on Tuesday afternoon. I brought her something shiny. This was what the gift guide in the magazine said ladies like. I'd lifted it from the shop where I'd seen her advert. I pulled flowers from gardens as I passed, but Isa was there, not Helen. Isa said, "Hello my name is Claudia." I paid, stripped and lay down. She swished her long dyed ponytail over my body. She unbuttoned her nurse's coat and swung out her dumbbell breasts, straddled me and lowered herself so they bulged against my chest. The whole of her was flattened against me at a right angle like she'd dropped there from the ceiling, like she'd overbalanced, and couldn't get up again. I could feel air between us in the gap underneath her breasts. The rest was sweaty. We unpeeled.

Isa said if I wanted to see her or Helen again I should go away for a long time. I said, should I complete three tasks? The tasks would be hard, I knew. But I am lucky, and in the end they were easy. I came back anyway.

There was a little old man helped me, and a donkey. I thought it should talk, but it didn't, however I tried to make it. But those bits are for other stories. Like the youngest sons in fairytales, I treated them to what they seemed to ask for, so that when I asked them for help again they did exactly what I told them to.

In the high street there were lights. On the chimney pot of the flat above the chemist, a Santa, lit from inside, ready to plunge. I walked past the Christmas houses with the lights on, boxes in different shapes, all designed to keep something in, or out. You could scream here and they'd never notice; or maybe they would: it's only bricks and mortar. All those boxes, all close together, all built to be the best shape to capture happiness. Did any of them work?

When I returned to Helen, she asked me to cut off her head, and I did it. Isa held her down and I used an axe from the hardware store where I'd also seen an astrology 2005 decorative dish still hopefully for sale. I could have gone for a saw, but it was the axe I lifted for her. I think she was meant to transform but I can't think what into: she was already a woman. I think we were meant to get married or something, after, and that showers of gold would pour from the wound, but nothing happened. Nothing except what you'd expect.

I'm not very good with words. I use them here but often they can't get out. I'm trying to tell you what it was – to cut into this thing that should be sacred, that thing we can't question, to make it just a thing like any other – which is what it becomes when you cut into it, when you cut it off. This is the moment the good things happen in stories, but this is real life. She was meant to change into something else. But she did. I looked into both of the parts of Helen that were left after, but neither of them answered.

So I didn't get a fortune this time. But I am the youngest son, and a boy. Luck follows me, Simple Hans.

In any case, I'd only come for the week.

ME AND THE FAT WOMAN – JOANNA WALSH

Since black holes by their very definition cannot be directly observed, proving their existence is difficult. The strongest evidence for black holes comes from binary systems in which a visible star can be shown to be orbiting a massive but unseen companion.

I can't remember when she appeared, or how I entered her orbit, but in the beginning we were quite chummy. The fat woman sat squarely on her patch. I sidled in from the sidelines. She offered me something from her basket. It was I who had solicited the acquaintance, although, had I known anything about her, it would have been obvious this is what she'd immediately have done.

Food is so expensive here (to import it over such distances!) that it's cheaper to bring some from home. I always had so much to carry that I brought very little, and so remained thin. The fat woman was stronger than me. Her basket was bigger. It tested her muscles, and what was in it sustained her. Though she gave from it freely, it did not seem ever to run out and, because she proffered, I asked for more. That seemed to be the way things went. I gave her as much pleasure by taking as she did me by giving, or so I reasoned. Oh we had some good times, me and the fat woman: picnics by the side of the road (I, always anxious that the basket from which she distributed might run dry, she never telling me what was in it, or how much was left).

Each day, at 4 o'clock, the fat woman took tea. You could set your watch by her as you passed and, in fact, that's what all of us did, though I – being increasingly close to her – had no need to do more than peer over at her wrist's large dial, losing only milliseconds in the glancing. Time went slow there. She unfolded her folding chair which, naturally, she had brought with her and, when she sat, time gathered round her like a picnic rug. I perched on her event horizon, hardly making a dent in it, never relaxing enough to cross the line, or so I thought. I looked at my own watch, which seemed to tick at the normal rate. She unfolded today's newspaper from 1919.

(The fat woman liked to keep up to date.)

It said:

"LIGHTS ALL ASKEW IN THE HEAVENS . . . BUT NOBODY NEED WORRY"

She had such gravity, she could only be behind *The Times*. Each time I looked across the space between us, I looked back. Light followed her, as she sat in the groove she had made. You might have said she was an angel in her setting with all she brought of out her basket arranged around her: her Le Creuset, her Le Chameaus, her Illy, her Bridgewater, her Falke, and those things she got from Lidl only you'd never have known it. Putting stuff into space-time bends it further, and objects may interact with one another, but the stuff that fell into her, we never saw again. A lot of it was stuff I'd never seen before, such as Vacherin, samphire, sourdough, celeriac, strings of spaghetti she said she'd made herself, and – although she simultaneously disapproved – occasional whole tubs of foie gras. 'Is that Danish Blue?' I asked. 'Dolcelatte,' she replied. Due to gravitational time dilation, we never even saw these things disappear. When I asked where they went, she dismissed my question. 'Things tend,' she said, 'towards a state of disorder, but why waste energy over it?' She laughed, continued to take things lightly. I, having only my own universe's sense of causality, absorbed this information carefully, reproduced it until it became me, until I became the Le Creuset, the Falke, the Vacherin, the foie gras, the Le Chameaus, or so you would have thought.

That I was not fat was not a problem, oh no not at all. She knew that I was not like the other thin women. Although insubstantial, it was obvious I was on her side. As for wanting to be thin, the fat woman was above all that. She preferred to reach out to those who were less significant than her, or, at least, she attracted them. Some took offence at her offers, others took what she offered, chagrined. Each time she reached out, the insignificant got further and further away from her, so she knew less and less about them. She thought I was insignificant, and I did not disabuse her, as, indeed, I was. But I was the only one who stayed by her, admiring her mass, and the things she produced, never-endingly, from her basket, including the production of space and time, which she placed between herself and everyone else (except me).

In order to bridge the gap between herself and the others, the fat woman began to take up more and more space. To accommodate her, I pared myself down further, until I was practically flat, then hardly more than one-dimensional. I stripped myself of the word righteous, and the word . . . well, all the words, until I wasn't feeling myself any more, until I was numb, uncalled for, but she had no need to call me: I was always there. Minus these words I looked no different. She didn't notice they had ever been attached to me. Lighter without them, she was able to lift me with her strong arms, pulling me out of ditches, setting me back on the side of the road. Sometimes I am frightened that the fat woman will kill me. But I'm stuck with her now, pressed here against her side, enfolded in her folds. It keeps me warm, at least.

The fat woman expanded because I let her, made room for her, clearing not only myself but the others away, whenever someone needed putting in their place, had overstepped the mark. And so she bulged far beyond hers, or at least beyond the mark of one person. Soon, her rotating body was everywhere in space, if you looked back far enough. Really, the arrogance of the fat woman. That she was so much more solid than I, that everything about her carried more weight. There had begun to be periods of quiescence between us: whether hers or mine, I don't know. I'd started to grow beyond her, or at least that's what I'd thought, though I can only see things from my perspective. From elsewhere in the universe, the whole thing may have looked entirely different. It depends how you understand the direction of time, which, to the eye, is not reversible.

No one really thought that she was pregnant, though some offered the word. 'You're not fat,' I told her. 'In fact I'm probably fatter than you are, relatively.' I didn't mean it, but suddenly I was. I'd worn sweatpants, hadn't noticed how I'd grown to fit them, tight. Had I really expanded? And how? Our relationship, though relatively speaking nothing special, was perhaps more binary than I'd thought, though I was only ever an ordinary companion, absorbing things from the fat woman, even turns of phrase, even facial expressions until, sometimes, when I peered into the mirror all I reflected was her. I absorbed so much that I wondered, sometimes, whether she could be in there too along with her Le Creuset, her Falke, her Vacherin, her Le Chameaus, her samphire, her Illy, her sourdough and her Bridgewater. Did we get too close? I can't determine. Depends on who you think was denser, and gravitational collapse produces great density; perhaps it was I who drew her in, in the end.

There is a finite amount of mass in the universe, or so it seems, but the space between objects may become infinite. The forces holding us together were no more than local, and I never was from round here. But these are not experiments we can do on earth. Those were different times, and *autres temps, autres mœurs.* Even proving her existence now is difficult, as most claim never to have seen her, though some remember seeing me, and knowing she could not be far off. But no one really knew what was going on with her, why she dressed her curves in black, for instance. They say it's slimming . . . well, it's no good looking for stable solutions. Right now she seems almost vanishingly small, as though seen through the wrong end of a telescope, or as if I were looking from the other end of time. It's almost as though she'd evaporated. I wish I'd a picture to remember her by, one of her sitting in the midst of it all, at the point of her singularity which was not, after all, perhaps, so singular, but always looked so to me, coming, as I did, from an entirely different universe. Still, taking a photo's never outside the realms of probability: move a little backwards, a little more . . . after all, you could photograph the Big Bang if you stood back far enough.

READING HABITS

H writes books for people who know more about maths than her, for the few people who know more about linguistics, and for general readers who may expect anything or nothing.

S is clever and well-educated but a bad reader. SL is a good reader but badly educated. g is better educated but a bad reader, and not so clever either.

None of them will read books by H.

W used to read novels but now reads, almost exclusively, biographies and histories. W is married to M, who went through a period a few years ago, around when her children were born, when she read only fashion magazines. Although she is now an accomplished reader tackling Dostoyevsky, Lacan, Foucault, she feels she should not miss issues of the fashion magazines and must read these too.

B's husband, g, dictates what B reads. She likes to read what he buys and does not think of it as dictation, but she never buys a book for herself. Sometimes B chooses books from libraries but, as the books will not continue to live with her, she does not see this as rebellion. g sees himself as an independent reader: he buys all of the books on the literary prize lists.

P, who is married to SL, reads detective stories, comic fantasy, and books about people who were young at the same time as he was young. The latter are biographies or autobiographies.

When O offers P a book, he feels strangely insulted.

F, who is married to S, reads the same kind of books as S, but not at her instigation.

At the end of each book, because both are intelligent, each is mystified by his or her disappointment. Still they continue to read.

L reads books for work. She is a writer. She enjoys reading them, but they are for work too. L is careful with her reading diet and feels bloated by books she does not like, or which do not contribute to her work. L reads books in one language. M reads books in two languages, N (L's husband) in three. O can read books in four. All the rest read books in one.

The children of H, W and M, L and N, F and S, read batches of similar books designed for children of their respective ages. Next year, they will move onto the next batch.

The children of g and B are grown up. One of them

is married to S. The children of P and SL are grown up. One of them is O.

O reads the same book again and again, sitting in the small bedroom he still occupies in his parents' house.

L, M, N and O would all read books by H. M has read one of H's books; N, two plus an unpublished manuscript which he is reviewing for a literary journal. The others have not actually read any books by H but mean to, except O, who would not. M once asked W to read a book by H but he refused and she felt a surprising sense of personal rejection.

None of the other people mentioned would read books by H.

HAUPTBAHNHOF

Two-way propositions: in the first example, the prepositional phrase describes a destination. In the second, it describes a location. German indicates this distinction through the use of cases (wohin/where to? wo/where at?).

I know what you are thinking.

But it is possible to sleep on the station.

If you don't look like you are homeless, if you change your clothes with reasonable regularity, above all if you look like you are waiting for someone.

I have perfected the waiting look.

After all, even if I am no longer sure whether I am waiting, or whether I only wish to appear to be waiting, it is my responsibility not to cause a 'situation', an incident. It is my responsibility to protect the people who pass through the station from the sight of a woman alone who is not waiting for anyone. Although, of course, I am.

And there is no better place to wait than the Hauptbahnhof. It is large enough for me to change platforms regularly. It is clean. There are vastly fewer pigeons than in any other grand central station in Europe.

The Hauptbahnhof smells of coffee, of floor polish, of cigarettes, of the substances we use to correct, to mark time, to keep ourselves together. Of course smoking is banned but this is difficult to police. Before they board their train, people will always want a last cigarette.

I pride myself on travelling light. Waiting, it is necessary to look as if you are expecting an arrival, or as if you are about to depart: conversely you must change platforms with reasonable regularity if you are to avoid the attention of the authorities. For both of these purposes, a small, light suitcase is ideal.

The Hauptbahnhof is open 24/7. Coincidences arrive at any time of day or night. I have become used to the sound of trains. There are two noises: the solid hum of the wheels on the track, and the lighter rattle of the upper parts of the rolling stock. Sometimes it seems laughable that they coincide.

Naturally I was disappointed you did not meet me. When I arrived I searched for you on the platform, thinking you had missed me in the crowd, had got the wrong Level. After a while I realised this was unlikely: the Signs mean that it is impossible to miss a train. If you know how to read the Signs, that is.

That night, I had trouble with the Signs. When I didn't see you I decided you must be waiting at your apartment. Perhaps there had been a confusion, or an engagement you had failed to mention. You had not sent your address but, knowing the name of your U-Bahn stop, I went to the stationer's on Level 0. At the stand with tourist books I dismissed the maps showing Berlin page by page. I needed to know where you were and where I was at the same time. I needed to see the whole city.

I slipped a map from its plastic compartment at the back of a city guide. Berlin was bigger than I expected. The map unfolded and unfolded until, under its own weight, it collapsed against itself, a long tear snaking across its centre.

The sound was deafening.

I had intended to steal the map having, surely, more need of it than anyone else. But the noise embarrassed me so much that I quickly refolded and stuffed it back into its plastic envelope.

I walked from the station a short distance across Europaplatz to steps leading down into the mouth of what looked like the underground. At the end of a white tunnel, I came upon two platforms, both empty, their Signs describing stops I did not recognise from the U-Bahn map. I took an up escalator, hoping for further platforms, but found myself back under the crystal dome of the station.

It was only later that I discovered the U-Bahn is not yet connected to the Hauptbahnhof.

Of course I did not then speak German.

But I have improved (you would be proud).

The Level 1 branch of Relay contains magazines from fifteen different countries. There are also phrase books, dictionaries and newspapers. It is possible, with time on your hands, to learn a language.

That first night I called you a couple of times but you didn't answer. It's possible I got your number wrong. I emailed you regarding this but you did not reply. I thought perhaps you were playing games, that you would relent or that, when we met, you would provide some good reason. Maybe it was a joke. I thought your phone was out of charge, that you had no connection. I thought you had lost it, that it had been stolen. I thought you were busy, were unavoidably detained, would answer later. I thought you had been arrested or were in hospital. I thought you were dead. There were so many possible explanations: I saw no reason not to hope.

In the meantime my diet is not what I might have wished but it is not expensive. As portions are large, it is possible to buy food only once each 24 hours and there is variety. I have become familiar with international cuisine and each day I choose my destination.

Dunkin' Donuts has the cheapest coffee, Starbucks the most expensive. They are virtually next door to each other, separated only by the hairdresser. This is not the sort of hairdresser I would normally visit – the type of place with posters of women whose hair is bleached and artificially stiff – but it is necessary to keep up appearances as we may meet at any time. With care, a blow-dry lasts all week, after which there is dry shampoo.

You might think have I regretted my light packing and tired of my single lipstick but the station's selection of cosmetic outlets and chemists means I can try a new shade every day. Sometimes a demonstrator makes me over to look like someone new. For the same reason, my skin has never looked better. I hear that changing your regime regularly renders products more effective (I have become up-to-date with the latest skincare developments). Sometime deodorising can be a problem but, if you don't mind using the spray kind with CFCs, you can generally get a squirt while the assistant is looking the other way.

Do I miss home? How would I? On the highest Level there is a shop with things for houses. Lifelike plastic dummies sit in deckchairs in the window. Everything is new, perfect. Things are bought and taken away and replaced by new new things. Nothing in the Hauptbahnhof ever wears out.

You would have thought the shop girls might recognise me after all this time, but they never do, only at the hairdressers where my details are on file so I get my regular stylist.

So many people pass through here . . .

The one difficulty is recharging my phone. I'm telling you this so you know why I cannot always be in touch. Not wanting to draw attention to my waiting, I am reluctant to ask in shops or at the ticket office, and am only occasionally able to clandestinely use the socket in Relay which, I presume, is for powering the vacuum cleaner.

How do I continue to support myself? Yes I know what you are thinking – but no need for that. I am not penniless. I do not have to pay for accommodation. My funds are not infinite. However I am economical, and I do not expect to wait forever.

I resent that I have to pay for water.

Using the dictionaries, the newspapers, the phrase books, I have arrived in my studies at German prepositions of time and place: nach (to/after/towards/by and still), and jetzt (up to/now/not yet and only just).

It is only sometimes that I think you are, perhaps, not still living in Berlin.

I heard you were in Edinburgh, a city where the station sits in a cleft between two green banks, its rails going merely forwards and back. From the street you look down on lines which braid but do not cross. There are no right angles – no Levels – only one long track into Scotland and another into England.

If you are in Edinburgh, you will have to return. I know you may take a plane but I understand a line will soon connect Hauptbahnhof to the airport. I can wait. Yes, there are buses, but that's not your style. If you have become famous in Scotland, there is always the possibility you may take a taxi, but I think it unlikely.

I prefer Departures to Arrivals, by which time everything has already happened. Even as dawn approaches in long lozenges of broken light, Arrivals do not notice the beautiful station. They look down, headed for something known, for home, for bed. Of course some are met, but fewer than you would think, and they don't stick around. Heroics are reserved for Departures: brave looks, last embraces, minutes slowed by kisses.

Surely everyone who lives in Berlin must pass through the Hauptbahnhof. It is only a matter of time.

Soon they will build the U-Bahn link. In the meantime I will wait at Arrivals. If I read the Signs correctly, as I now can, I will not miss a single one.

It is good to know exactly where you are.

Dear readers,

As well as relying on bookshop sales, And Other Stories relies on subscriptions from people like you for many of our books, whose stories other publishers often consider too risky to take on.

Our subscribers don't just make the books physically happen. They also help us approach booksellers, because we can demonstrate that our books already have readers and fans. And they give us the security to publish in line with our values, which are collaborative, imaginative and 'shamelessly literary'.

All of our subscribers:

- receive a first-edition copy of each of the books they subscribe to
- are thanked by name at the end of our subscriber-supported books
- receive little extras from us by way of thank you, for example: postcards created by our authors

BECOME A SUBSCRIBER, OR GIVE A SUBSCRIPTION TO A FRIEND

Visit andotherstories.org/subscribe to help make our books happen. You can subscribe to books we're in the process of making. To purchase books we have already published, we urge you to support your local or favourite bookshop and order directly from them – the often unsung heroes of publishing.

OTHER WAYS TO GET INVOLVED

If you'd like to know about upcoming events and reading groups (our foreign-language reading groups help us choose books to publish, for example) you can:

- join the mailing list at: andotherstories.org/join-us
- follow us on Twitter: @andothertweets
- join us on Facebook: facebook.com/AndOtherStoriesBooks
- follow our blog: andotherstoriespublishing.tumblr.com

This book was made possible thanks to the support of:

Aaron McEnery · Aaron Schneider · Abdullah Chowdhury · Ada Gokay · Adam Barnard · Adam Bowman · Adam Butler · Adam Lenson · Adriana Diaz Enciso · Aileen-Elizabeth Taylor · Ailsa Peate · Ajay Sharma · Alastair Gillespie · Alastair Laing · Alex Fleming · Alex Hancock · Alex Ramsey · Alexandra de Verseg-Roesch · Ali Smith · Alice Fischer · Alice Nightingale · Alice Ramsey · Alice Toulmin · Alison Hughes · Alison Layland · Alison MacConnell · Allison Graham · Alyse Ceirante · Amanda · Amanda Harvey · Amber Da · Amelia Dowe · Ami Zarchi · Amy Rushton · Ana Hincapie · Andrea Reece · Andrew Lees · Andrew Marston · Andrew McDougall · Andrew Reece · Andrew Rego · Angela Creed · Angus Walker · Anna Corrigan · Anna McKee-Poore · Anna Milsom · Anna Ruehl · Anna Vaught · Anne Carus · Anne Guest · Anne Ryden · Annette Hamilton · Annie McDermott · Anonymous · Anonymous · Anonymous · Anonymous · Anthony Brown · Anton Muscatelli · Antonia Lloyd-Jones · Antonia Saske · Antonio de Swift · Antony Pearce · Archie Davies · Arwen Smith · Asako Serizawa · Asher Norris · Ashley Hamilton · Audrey Mash · Avril Marren · Barbara & Terry Feller · Barbara Mellor · Beatriz St. John · Becky Woolley · Belynder Walia · Ben Schofield · Ben Thornton · Benjamin Judge · Bernard Devaney · Beth Hancock · Bev Thomas · Beverly Jackson · Bianca Duec · Bianca Jackson · Bianca Winter · Bill Fletcher · Blythe Ridge Sloan · Branka Maricic · Brenda Sully · Brendan McIntyre · Briallen Hopper · Brigita Ptackova · Caitlin Halpern · Caitlyn Chappell · Caitriona Lally · Candida Lacey · Caren Harple · Carla Carpenter · Carol Laurent · Carolina Pineiro · Caroline Paul · Caroline Picard · Caroline Rucker · Caroline Waight · Caroline West · Cassidy Hughes · Catherine Barton · Catherine Mansfield · Catherine Taylor · Catriona Gibbs · Cecilia Rossi · Cecilia Uribe · Cecily Maude · Charles Raby · Charlie Laing · Charlotte Holtam · Charlotte Murrie & Stephen Charles · Charlotte Whittle · Cheryl Maude · China Miéville · Chris Ames · Chris Lintott · Chris McCann · Chris Nielsen · Chris Stevenson · Chris & Kathleen Repper-Day · Christina Moutsou · Christine Brantingham · Christine Ebdy · Christine Luker · Christopher Allen · Ciara Ní Riain · Claire Brooksby · Claire Malcolm · Claire Tristram · Claire Williams · Clare Archibald · Clare Young · Clarissa Botsford · Claudia Hoare · Claudia Nannini · Clifford Posner · Clive Bellingham · Colin Burro w · Colin Matthews · Courtney Lilly · Craig Barney · Dan Walpole · Dana Behrman · Daniel Arnold · Daniel Gillespie · Daniel Hahn · Daniel Rice · Daniel Stewart · Daniel Sweeney · Daniel Venn · Daniela Steierberg · Darcy Hurford · Dave Lander · Dave Young · Davi Rocha · David Anderson · David Finlay · David Gavin · David Gould · David Hebblethwaite · David Higgins · David Johnson-Davies · David Jones · David Roberts · David Shriver · David Smith · David Steege · David Travis · Dawn Leonard · Debbie Pinfold · Deirdre Nic Mhathuna · Denis Stillewagt & Anca Fronescu · Denise Muir · Diana Fox Carney · Dinah Bourne · Dominick Santa Cattarina · Duncan Clubb · Ed Owles · Edward Haxton · Edward Rathke · Elaine Kennedy · Elaine Rassaby · Eleanor Dawson · Eleanor Maier · Elie Howe · Elina Zicmane · Elisabeth Cook · Elise Gilbert · Eliza O'Toole · Elizabeth Heighway · Ellen Coopersmith ·

Ellen Kennedy · Ellen Wilkinson · Ellie Goddard · Elly Zelda Goldsmith · Emily Chia & Marc Ronnie · Emily Taylor · Emily Williams · Emily Yaewon Lee & Gregory Limpens · Emma Bielecki · Emma Perry · Emma Pope · Emma Yearwood · Emma Louise Grove · Eric E Rubeo · Erin Grace Cobby · Eva Kostyu · Ewan Tant · Fawzia Kane · Finbarr Farragher · Finlay McEwan · Finnuala Butler · Florian Duijsens · Fran Sanderson · Frances Hazelton · Francesca Brooks · Francesca Fanucci · Francis Taylor · Francisco Vilhena · Frank van Orsouw · Freya Warren · Friederike Knabe · Gabriela Lucia Garza de Linde · Gabrielle Crockatt · Gale Pryor · Gary Gorton · Gavin Collins · Gavin Smith · Gawain Espley · Gemma Tipton · Geoff Thrower · Geoffrey Cohen · Geoffrey Urland · George Christie · George Wilkinson · Gerard Mehigan · Gill Boag-Munroe · Gillian Ackroyd · Gillian Bohnet · Gillian Grant · Gordon Cameron · Graham Duff · Graham R Foster · Grant Hartwell · Grant Rintoul · GRJ Beaton · Hadil Balzan · Hank Pryor · Hannah Jones · Hannah Mayblin · Hannah Richter · Hannah Stevens · Hans Lazda · Harriet Spicer · Heather Tipon · Helen Asquith · Helen Barker · Helen Brady · Helen Snow · Helen Swain · Helen Weir · Helen White · Helen Wormald · Henrike Laehnemann · Henry Asson · HL Turner-Heffer · Howard Robinson · Hugh Gilmore · Iain Munro · Ian Barnett · Ian McMillan · Ian Randall · Ingrid Olsen · Irene Mansfield · Isabel Adey · Isabella Garment · Isabella Weibrecht · Istvan Szatmari · J Collins · Jack Brown · Jacqueline Haskell · Jacqueline Lademann · Jacqueline Ting Lin · James Attlee · James Butcher · James Cubbon · James Lesniak · James Portlock · James Scudamore · James Tierney · James Wilper · Jamie Mollart · Jamie Walsh · Jane Leuchter · Jane Livingstone · Jane Woollard · Janette Ryan · Janika Urig · Jasmine Gideon · JC Sutcliffe · Jean Pierre de Rosnay · Jean-Jacques Regouffre · Jeanne Wilson · Jeehan Quijano · Jeff Collins · Jennifer Bernstein · Jennifer Higgins · Jennifer O'Brien · Jenny Huth · Jenny Newton · Jenny Nicholls · Jenny Yang · Jeremy Weinstock · Jess Howard-Armitage · Jethro Soutar · Jillian Jones · Jo Bell · Jo Bellamy · Jo Harding · Jo Lateu · Joanna Flower · Joanna Luloff · Joao Pedro Bragatti Winckler · Jodie Adams · Jodie Hare · Joel Love · Joelle Delbourgo · Joelle Skilbeck · Johan Forsell · Johan Trouw · Johannes Georg Zipp · John Berube · John Conway · John Down · John Gent · John Hartley · John Hodgson · John Kelly · John McGill · John McKee · John Royley · John Shaw · John Steigerwald · John Winkelman · Jon Talbot · Jonathan Blaney · Jonathan Ruppin · Jonathan Watkiss · Joseph Camilleri · Joseph Cooney · Joseph Huennekens · Joseph Schreiber · Joseph Zanella · Joshua Davis · Joshua McNamara · Judith Virginia Moffatt · Judyth Emanuel · Julia Hays · Julia Hobsbawm · Julia Hoskins · Julia Rochester · Julian Duplain · Julian Lomas · Julie Gibson · Julie Gibson · JW Mersky · Kaarina Hollo · Kapka Kassabova · Karen Waloschek · Karl Chwe · Karl Kleinknecht & Monika Motylinska · Kasper Haakansson · Kasper Hartmann · Kate Attwooll · Kate Griffin · Katharina Herzberger · Katharine Freeman · Katharine Robbins · Katherine El-Salahi · Katherine Green · Katherine Mackinnon · Katherine Parish · Katherine Sotejeff-Wilson · Kathleen Magone · Kathryn Edwards · Kathryn Lewis · Katie Brown · Katrina Thomas · Katriona Macpherson · Keith Walker · Kirsteen Smith · Kirsten Major · KL Ee · Klara Rešetič · Krystine Phelps · Kuaam Animashaun · Lana

Selby · Lander Hawes · Laura Batatota · Laura Clarke · Laura Lea · Laura Waddell · Lauren Ellemore · Laurence Laluyaux · Leanne Bass · Leigh Vorhies · Leonie Schwab · Leonie Smith · Leri Price · Lesley Lawn · Lesley Watters · Leslie Wines · Liliana Lobato · Linda Walz · Lindsay Brammer · Lindsey Ford · Lindy van Rooyen · Liz Clifford · Liz Sage · Lizzi Thomson · Lizzie Broadbent · Lizzie Coulter · LJ Nicolson · Lochlan Bloom · Lola Boorman · Loretta Platts · Lorna Bleach · Lorna Scott Fox · Lottie Smith · Louisa Hare · Louise Curtin · Louise Musson · Louise Piper · Luc Verstraete · Lucia Rotheray · Lucy Caldwell · Lucy Hariades · Lucy Moffatt · Lucy Phillips · Luke Healey · Lynda Graham · Lynn Martin · M Manfre · Madeline Teevan · Maeve Lambe · Maggie Livesey · Mal Campbell · Mandy Wight · Manja Pflanz · Marcella Morgan · Marcus Joy · Marie Donnelly · Marina Castledine · Marja S Laaksonen · Mark Lumley · Mark Sargent · Mark Sztyber · Mark Waters · Martha Gifford · Martha Nicholson · Martha Stevns · Martin Boddy · Martin Brampton · Martin Price · Martin Vosyka · Martin Whelton · Mary Carozza · Mary Wang · Marzieh Youssefi · Matt Klein · Matt & Owen Davies · Matthew Black · Matthew Francis · Matthew Geden · Matthew Smith · Matthew Thomas · Matthew Warshauer · Matty Ross · Maureen Pritchard · Max Cairnduff · Max Longman · Meaghan Delahunt · Megan Taylor · Megan Wittling · Melissa Beck · Melissa Quignon-Finch · Meredith Jones · Meredith Martin · Michael Aguilar · Michael Andal · Michael Johnston · Michael Ward · Michele Keyaert · Michelle Lotherington · Miranda Persaud · Mitchell Albert · Molly Foster · Monika Olsen · Morag Campbell · Morven Dooner · Myles Nolan · N Jabinh · Namita Chakrabarty · Nancy Oakes · Natalie Smith · Nathalie Adams · Nathalie Atkinson · Neil Pretty · Nicholas Brown · Nick James · Nick Nelson & Rachel Eley · Nick Sidwell · Nick Williams · Nicola Hart · Nicola Sandiford · Nicole Matteini · Nigel Palmer · Nikolaj Ramsdal Nielsen · Nina Alexandersen · Nina Moore · Noah Levin · Octavia Kingsley · Olivia Payne · Pam Madigan · Pashmina Murthy · Pat Crowe · Patricia Hughes · Patrick McGuinness · Patrick Owen · Paul Bailey · Paul Cray · Paul Howe & Ally Hewitt · Paul Jones · Paul Munday · Paul Robinson · Paula Edwards · Paula McGrath · Penelope Hewett Brown · Peter McCambridge · Peter Rowland · Peter Vos · Philip Carter · Philip Warren · Phyllis Reeve · Piet Van Bockstal · PM Goodman · PRAH Foundation · Rachael Williams · Rachel Bambury · Rachel Beddow · Rachel Gregory · Rachel Hinkel · Rachel Lasserson · Rachel Matheson · Rachel Parkin · Rachel Van Riel · Rachel Wadham · Rachel Watkins · Read MAW Books · Rebecca Braun · Rebecca Moss · Rebecca Roadman · Rebecca Rosenthal · Rebekah Hughes · Réjane Collard-Walker · Renee Humphrey · Rhiannon Armstrong · Rhodri Jones · Richard Ashcroft · Richard Bauer · Richard Ellis · Richard Gwyn · Richard Mansell · Richard Priest · Richard Shea · Richard Shore · Richard Soundy · Rishi Dastidar · Rita Hynes · RM Foord · Robert Downing · Robert Gillett · Robert Hugh-Jones · Robert Norman · Robin Patterson · Robin Taylor · Rory Williamson · Ros Schwartz · Rosanna Foster · Rose Arnold · Roz Simpson · Rupert Ziziros · Ruth Parkin · S Altinel · S Italiano · S Wight · Sabrina Uswak · Sally Baker · Sam Gordon · Sam Norman · Sam Ruddock · Samantha Smith · Sandra Neilson · Sarah Arboleda · Sarah Benson · Sarah Butler · Sarah Duguid · Sarah Lippek · Sarah Lucas · Sarah

Pybus · Sarah Wollner · Sasha Dugdale · Scott Thorough · Sean Malone · Sean McGivern · Sez Kiss · Shannon Knapp · Shawn Moedl · Sheridan Marshall · Shira Lob · Shirley Harwood · Sian Rowe · Sigurjon Sigurdsson · Silvia Kwon · Simon Robertson · Sioned Puw Rowlands · SJ Bradley · SK Grout · Sofia Hardinger · Sonia Crites · Sonia Overall · Sophie Bowley-Aicken · Sophie Goldsworthy · Sophy Roberts · ST Dabbagh · Stacy Rodgers · Stefanie Barschdorf · Stefanie May IV · Stephan Eggum · Stephanie Lacava · Stephen Coade · Stephen Pearsall · Steven & Gitte Evans · Stuart Wilkinson · Sue Little · Sue & Ed Aldred · Susan Ferguson · Susan Higson · Susan Irvine · Susie Roberson · Suzanne Fortey · Suzanne Lee · Suzy Ceulan Hughes · Swannee Welsh · Tamar Shlaim · Tamara Larsen · Tammi Owens · Tammy Harman · Tammy Watchorn · Tania Hershman · Ted Burness · Teresa Griffiths · Terry Kurgan · The Mighty Douche Softball Team · Thees Spreckelsen · Thomas Bell · Thomas Chadwick · Thomas Fritz · Thomas Mitchell · Thomas van den Bout · Tiffany Lehr · Tim Theroux · Timothy Harris · Tina Rother-ham-Winqvist · Toby Ryan · Tom Darby · Tom Franklin · Tom Gray · Tom Wilbey · Tony Bastow · Torna Russell-Hills · Tory Jeffay · Tracy Shapley · Trevor Lewis · Trevor Wald · Tricia Durdey · Val Challen · Vanessa Dodd · Vanessa Jones · Vanessa Nolan · Vanessa Rush · Victor Meadow-croft · Victoria Adams · Victoria Seaman · Vijay Pattisapu · Vilis Kasims · Virginia Weir · Visaly Muthusamy · Wendy Langridge · Wendy Peate · Wenna Price · Will Huxter · William Dennehy · William Mackenzie · William Schwaber · Zoe Stephenson · Zoe Taylor · Zoë Brasier

Current & Upcoming Books

01

Juan Pablo Villalobos, *Down the Rabbit Hole*
translated from the Spanish by Rosalind Harvey

02

Clemens Meyer, *All the Lights*
translated from the German by Katy Derbyshire

03

Deborah Levy, *Swimming Home*

04

Iosi Havilio, *Open Door*
translated from the Spanish by Beth Fowler

05

Oleg Zaionchkovsky, *Happiness is Possible*
translated from the Russian by Andrew Bromfield

06

Carlos Gamerro, *The Islands*
translated from the Spanish by Ian Barnett

07

Christoph Simon, *Zbinden's Progress*
translated from the German by Donal McLaughlin

08

Helen DeWitt, *Lightning Rods*

09

Deborah Levy, *Black Vodka: ten stories*

10

Oleg Pavlov, *Captain of the Steppe*
translated from the Russian by Ian Appleby

11

Rodrigo de Souza Leão, *All Dogs are Blue*
translated from the Portuguese by Zoë Perry & Stefan Tobler

12

Juan Pablo Villalobos, *Quesadillas*
translated from the Spanish by Rosalind Harvey

13

Iosi Havilio, *Paradises*
translated from the Spanish by Beth Fowler

14

Ivan Vladislavić, *Double Negative*

15

Benjamin Lytal, *A Map of Tulsa*

16

Ivan Vladislavić, *The Restless Supermarket*

17

Elvira Dones, *Sworn Virgin*
translated from the Italian by Clarissa Botsford

18

Oleg Pavlov, *The Matiushin Case*
translated from the Russian by Andrew Bromfield

19

Paulo Scott, *Nowhere People*
translated from the Portuguese by Daniel Hahn

20

Deborah Levy, *An Amorous Discourse in the Suburbs of Hell*

21

Juan Tomás Ávila Laurel, *By Night the Mountain Burns*
translated from the Spanish by Jethro Soutar

22

SJ Naudé, *The Alphabet of Birds*
translated from the Afrikaans by the author

23

Niyati Keni, *Esperanza Street*

24

Yuri Herrera, *Signs Preceding the End of the World*
translated from the Spanish by Lisa Dillman

25

Carlos Gamerro, *The Adventure of the Busts of Eva Perón*
translated from the Spanish by Ian Barnett

26

Anne Cuneo, *Tregian's Ground*
translated from the French by Roland Glasser
and Louise Rogers Lalaurie

27

Angela Readman, *Don't Try This at Home*

28

Ivan Vladislavić, *101 Detectives*

29

Oleg Pavlov, *Requiem for a Soldier*
translated from the Russian by Anna Gunin

30

Haroldo Conti, *Southeaster*
translated from the Spanish by Jon Lindsay Miles

31

Ivan Vladislavić, *The Folly*

32

Susana Moreira Marques, *Now and at the Hour of Our Death*
translated from the Portuguese by Julia Sanches

33

Lina Wolff, *Bret Easton Ellis and the Other Dogs*
translated from the Swedish by Frank Perry

34

Anakana Schofield, *Martin John*

35

Joanna Walsh, *Vertigo*

36

Wolfgang Bauer, *Crossing the Sea*
translated from the German by Sarah Pybus
with photographs by Stanislav Krupař

37

Various, *Lunatics, Lovers and Poets:*
Twelve Stories after Cervantes and Shakespeare

38

Yuri Herrera, *The Transmigration of Bodies*
translated from the Spanish by Lisa Dillman

39

César Aira, *The Seamstress and the Wind*
translated from the Spanish by Rosalie Knecht

40

Juan Pablo Villalobos, *I'll Sell You a Dog*
translated from the Spanish by Rosalind Harvey

41

Enrique Vila-Matas, *Vampire in Love*
translated from the Spanish by Margaret Jull Costa

42

Emmanuelle Pagano, *Trysting*
translated from the French by Jennifer Higgins and Sophie Lewis

43

Arno Geiger, *The Old King in His Exile*
translated from the German by Stefan Tobler

44

Michelle Tea, *Black Wave*

45

César Aira, *The Little Buddhist Monk*
translated from the Spanish by Nick Caistor

46

César Aira, *The Proof*
translated from the Spanish by Nick Caistor

47

Patty Yumi Cottrell, *Sorry to Disrupt the Peace*

48

Yuri Herrera, *Kingdom Cons*
translated from the Spanish by Lisa Dillman

49

Fleur Jaeggy, *I am the Brother of XX*
translated from the Italian by Gini Alhadeff

50

Iosi Havilio, *Petite Fleur*
translated from the Spanish by Lorna Scott Fox

51

Juan Tomás Ávila Laurel, *The Gurugu Pledge*
translated from the Spanish by Jethro Soutar

52

Joanna Walsh, *Worlds from the Word's End*

JOANNA WALSH is the author of *Vertigo*, *Hotel*, *Grow a Pair* and *Fractals*. Her writing has also been published in *Granta*, *The Dalkey Archive Best European Fiction 2015*, *Best British Short Stories* 2014 and 2015, *The Stinging Fly*, *gorse*, *The Dublin Review* and many more. She reviews for, amongst others, *The New Statesman* and *The Guardian*. She was a judge on the 2016 Goldsmiths Prize, is a contributing editor at *3:AM* magazine and Catapult, and is the founder of @read_women. She was awarded the 2017 UK Arts Foundation Fellowship in Creative Non-Fiction.